PQE329838

A Family
for a Week

MELISSA SENATE

Seven days to change the bachelor's ways...

HARLEQUIN
SPECIAL EDITION

**Believe in love. Overcome obstacles.
Find happiness.**

*Relate to finding comfort and strength in the
support of loved ones and enjoy the journey
no matter what life throws your way.*

AVAILABLE THIS MONTH

**IN SEARCH OF
THE LONG-LOST
MAVERICK**
CHRISTINE
RIMMER

**A MOTHER'S
SECRETS**
TARA TAYLOR
QUINN

**A FAMILY
FOR A WEEK**
MELISSA SENATE

BABY LESSONS
TERI WILSON

**HIS PLAN FOR THE
QUINTUPLETS**
CATHY GILLEN
THACKER

**MORE THAN
NEIGHBORS**
SHANNON STACEY

HSEATMIFC0720

Axel moved closer to her to leave the room—so that Danny could sleep in peace—but Sadie was right there, in the doorway, and suddenly they were kissing again.

"Why can't I keep my hands off you?" she whispered against his lips, pressed up tantalizingly against him.

"Feel free not to," he said, then regretted it. Even if he was attracted to her on a bunch of levels—okay, all—he wasn't getting emotionally attached.

She seemed to sense his withdrawal despite his not moving a muscle. "Maybe we should save the making out for when my family is around," she said, and he heard the element of disappointment in her voice. He was getting to know her a little too well. "You know, to make the engagement seem real. We were supposed to talk about that and never did. But now I'm zonked," she said, fake yawning again and backing toward her room. "So, see you in the morning."

She hurried down the hall, and her door closed a second later.

He could knock and they could talk, really talk. But his feet were suddenly weighted to the floor, and Sadie had fled for a reason. He should let her be.

Wasn't getting emotionally attached. Even he knew when he was full of it.

DAWSON FAMILY RANCH:
Life, love, legacy in Wyoming.

Dear Reader,

Ah, family reunions. The big, loud, loving Winston clan descends on the Dawson Family Guest Ranch for their annual weeklong family reunion in honor of Axel Dawson rescuing Sadie Winston's toddler son when he went missing recently. Axel is the new Winston family hero—and little Danny's.

Sadie was so grateful that Axel, a former search-and-rescue operative, found her missing son that she, too, fell a little bit in love with him the day he put her boy back in her arms on a Wyoming mountain. But she knows Axel Dawson is a confirmed bachelor who doesn't do love or commitment. Yet when her sister gets engaged during the reunion, and Sadie's ninety-nine-year-old great-grandmother mistakes Sadie for the bride and Axel for the groom, suddenly, the unlikely couple is pretending to be planning a wedding. Lots of surprises and love are in store for the Winstons and the Dawsons this week...

I hope you enjoy Sadie and Axel's story. Feel free to write me with any comments or questions at MelissaSenate@yahoo.com and visit my website, melissasenate.com for more info about me and my books. For lots of photos of my cat and dog, friend me over on Facebook.

Happy summer and happy reading!

Warmest regards,

Melissa Senate

A Family
for a Week

MELISSA SENATE

HARLEQUIN®
SPECIAL EDITION™

Recycling programs for this product may not exist in your area.

ISBN-13: 978-1-335-89465-6

A Family for a Week

Copyright © 2020 by Melissa Senate

All rights reserved. No part of this book may be used or reproduced in any manner whatsoever without written permission except in the case of brief quotations embodied in critical articles and reviews.

This is a work of fiction. Names, characters, places and incidents are either the product of the author's imagination or are used fictitiously. Any resemblance to actual persons, living or dead, businesses, companies, events or locales is entirely coincidental.

This edition published by arrangement with Harlequin Books S.A.

For questions and comments about the quality of this book, please contact us at CustomerService@Harlequin.com.

Harlequin Enterprises ULC
22 Adelaide St. West, 40th Floor
Toronto, Ontario M5H 4E3, Canada
www.Harlequin.com

Printed in U.S.A.

Melissa Senate has written many novels for Harlequin and other publishers, including her debut, *See Jane Date*, which was made into a TV movie. She also wrote seven books for Harlequin's Special Edition line under the pen name Meg Maxwell. Her novels have been published in over twenty-five countries. Melissa lives on the coast of Maine with her teenage son; their rescue shepherd mix, Flash; and a lap cat named Cleo. For more information, please visit her website, melissasenate.com.

For my sister.

Chapter One

Holding her twenty-seven-month-old son against one hip, single mom Sadie Winston—and thirty-eight of her relatives—walked around the outdoor petting zoo at the Dawson Family Guest Ranch. Little Danny stared wide-eyed at the goats jumping on and off a short log in the hay-strewn pen. One with bristly black fur came over to sniff Danny's sneaker. "'Oat, 'oat!" her son shouted with a giggle.

The whole clan had arrived a few minutes ago for their annual family reunion, the barn their first stop after check-in. As Danny laughed and pointed at the goats, Sadie looked in every direction—ever so casually, she hoped—for a certain tall, black-haired, blue-eyed man named Axel Dawson. He and his siblings owned the guest ranch, and she'd heard he lived on the property now. She didn't see him anywhere, and Axel Dawson would be impossible to miss.

"'Oat, Mama!" Danny said again, pointing at a white goat chewing on a piece of hay. Sadie set Danny down, smiling as the goat came over to nudge his hand for a pat or a treat. "'Oat, 'oat!"

She kneeled behind Danny and wrapped her arms around him, breathing in the baby-shampoo scent of his blond hair. She closed her eyes for a second, grateful. She'd almost lost him once. She *had* lost him—for over two hours. That she had him back was the whole reason her mother and aunt—reunion organizers for decades—had chosen to hold the event at the Dawson ranch. As a very expensive but priceless thank-you.

Three months ago, on a beautiful May afternoon, Danny had gone missing during a family outing on a small mountain in Badger Tree National Park. One minute, he'd been right there, toddling between her aunt and mother as they all ambled and chatted their way up the easy incline to a wide expanse of forest where they'd planned to stop for a picnic.

Sadie had been deep in conversation with Daphne, her pregnant cousin who was full of questions about impending motherhood, when she'd heard her mom say, "Where's Danny?" A second later, "Danny? Where are you, sweetie?" The four women had looked at each other, each expecting Danny to appear, but he was nowhere to be found.

Panic. They'd rushed in every direction, looking, calling his name. Nothing. Silence. The breeze through the treetops the only sound when they'd forced themselves to stop and listen.

Her mother was on the phone with 911 when Sadie emerged from behind a tree, shaking her head, tears streaming down her face. "Danny!" she'd called out as loud as she could, trying to keep the fear out of her voice so as not to scare him *if* he could hear her. Silence.

At footsteps, they'd all turned expectantly and rushed over, but it was a young couple with hiking poles. No, they hadn't seen a little boy with blond hair and orange light-up sneakers. Sorry. They'd help look, though, they'd said.

Converse County search and rescue, park rangers and local police were there within minutes. A tall, dark-haired man, his orange shirt emblazoned front and back with *Badger Tree National Park Search and Rescue*, *Axel Dawson* embroidered on the right chest, appeared with a dog, a yellow Lab, and asked for something with Danny's scent. Sadie pulled Danny's hoodie from her backpack, and Axel held it under the dog's nose, then stared at the photos of Danny on Sadie's phone. He'd had her text a few to him, and then he'd rushed into the woods near the last spot the women were sure they'd seen him. Two hours later, Danny was still lost, radios crackling, areas checked rattled off. Axel Dawson had reappeared to speak to Sadie, asking for special words Danny liked, songs he knew, and she'd been so out of her mind she'd barely remembered his favorite word was *nana*— for banana, not grandmother—and he liked the "Itsy Bitsy Spider" song.

Axel had put warm, strong hands on her shoulders, looked her right in the eyes with his startling blue ones and said, as the sun went down behind him, that he'd find her son. He'd said it with such conviction in his voice, in his expression, that she'd believed him more than she'd ever believed anything.

Twenty minutes later, the radios of the park ranger and police officer who'd stayed with the family had blared to life, and the ranger screamed, "Danny has been found! He's alive and well, and they're heading here!" Cheers went up among the group, including the EMTs at the ready. Sadie dropped to her knees with relief. Her mom, aunt and cousin were crying and staring in every direction, waiting. And then out of the tree line came Axel Dawson, his right cheek bleeding from a long scrape, holding Danny tight in his arms as the boy sang "Itsy Bitsy Spider" and made the spider hand gesture up to Axel's chin, the yellow Lab following them.

Sadie had gone flying over, sobbing *thank you* over and over as she'd reached out for Danny. She'd held her son close, covering him with kisses, and then the EMTs had led her over to the ambulance. Danny seemed okay but had his share of scratches. He'd been chasing a woodland critter and had ended up crawling through brush and vines into a well-hidden badger's den and fallen asleep. Dude, Axel's search and rescue K-9 partner, had sniffed him out and stayed put until Axel got in and got the boy out.

Sadie had heard this all secondhand from the police and EMTs, who'd heard it from Axel via radio when he'd been rushing the boy out of the woods. She'd looked for him to thank him again, but he appeared to be getting a serious dressing-down from another man in a park search and rescue shirt, and then she and her family had gone to the hospital to have Danny checked out, and she hadn't seen Axel Dawson again. She'd returned the next day, bringing a pie from her mother, a strudel from her aunt and a hundred-dollar gift card from her cousin to a local restaurant, but she'd heard he'd left town for a while.

Apparently, he'd broken a few rules to find Danny and had been sent home on enforced "rest and relaxation" for two weeks. Sadie had felt terrible about that. A couple of days later, when she'd gotten Axel's address and gone to his cabin nestled at the base of the mountain to thank him in person and apologize for whatever had happened, a fellow ranger had said that Axel had gone to his family's guest ranch out in Bear Ridge for a while. Sadie's mom had immediately tried to book their annual family reunion at the Dawson ranch, but there were no openings till winter—and the family needed all six cabins. A few days later, though, Sadie's mom had gotten a call from the Dawson ranch that a corporate retreat had canceled for the last week of August, and voilà: thirty-eight of Sadie's relatives had descended on the rural Wyoming property.

"Remember, he's single," her mother whispered into Sadie's ear.

Ugh. How did Viv Winston always know what she was doing? How could her mom possibly know that Sadie was thinking about Axel Dawson? Though technically, Sadie was thinking about what happened three months ago. The man was a huge part of that, though.

"Not *that* single," Sadie whispered. "I told you what the park ranger said."

Three of the rangers, two female and one male, had come to the hospital to visit Danny and bring him stuffed toys, which had been incredibly kind, and as they were leaving, Sadie had heard one say, "Is McGorgeous here?"

The other had said, "Give it up, already. I told you I heard Axel Dawson doesn't do commitment."

"I know, but I like to look at him," the other said, and they chuckled.

Sadie had filed that tidbit away. Axel *was* nice to look at, *and* he'd found her son and brought him to her. The combination was potent. The past few months, she'd had a passing thought or two or a hundred about getting to know him better while at the reunion on his ranch. But better to think of him as a superhero like her family did instead of a man she could actually get to know better. Sadie Winston did not, repeat, *did not* want anything to do with a man who didn't "do commitment."

"Oh flibberty-poop," Viv said with a wave of her arm, her ash-blond bob swinging by her chin. She smiled at two of the children who were following a chicken, then sidled closer to Sadie. "Everyone wants love."

Sadie sure did. A nutritionist specializing in geriatric patients for the Converse County General Hospital in Prairie City, which was a town over from Bear Ridge, Sadie had a rewarding job, a nice small house in the center of town, friends, a big family, but she was sick to death of showing up alone to weddings and family parties. She was fine on her own, sure. But she wanted her life's partner, dammit. Someone who'd care if she was running late. Someone to be there. Someone to wake up with, share her day with. Someone to share *life* with. Someone who'd love Danny the way she did. She'd married Danny's father after a whirlwind courtship, despite his telling her he'd never thought he'd be the settling-down kind. She'd believed he loved her so much that he'd change. But when she told him she was pregnant, he'd disappeared with the rodeo—faster than she could even fill out paperwork to change her last name. Ever since, Sadie's motto was *when someone tells you who they are, believe them*. Axel had made it clear to everyone he wasn't the settling-down sort either. She should believe it.

"Zul!" Danny shouted, pointing.

Sadie's heart sped up, and she glanced around. *Zul* was Danny's attempt at saying Axel. Thanks to her family referring to the man as the family hero for the past three months, Danny had turned one of his stuffed animals, a floppy yellow lion with a shaggy brown mane, into "Zul." Sadie's grandmother Vanessa had made a little red cape for the lion, and the hero worship was complete. It was Danny's lovey, and he took it everywhere. Sadie knew her aunt was holding it right now so that Danny could pet the animals. "When Zul?" Danny had asked every day as he flew the lion around.

Finally, Sadie had a real answer for him. Because as the little boy took off running past the goats toward the open barn door, Sadie watched a tall, dark-haired, ocean-eyed man in a Stetson stop dead in his tracks as her son sprinted straight for him.

Axel Dawson.

A toddler—two years old at most—in a straw cowboy hat was running full speed right at Axel. *Whoa there, little guy.* In about a minute, the tyke would collide with Axel's knees. And since Axel had almost done his left knee in this morning from rescuing Hermione, the ranch's famed runaway goat, from a narrow cliff up Clover Mountain just behind the ranch, he didn't think it could take twenty-five pounds of flying energy.

The hat flew off the boy's head, his mop of blond hair flopping as he sped toward Axel, who stood about twenty feet away near the barn door. Two women in their fifties hurried after the bolter.

Axel squinted in the bright sunshine. Holy molasses. Was that little Danny Winston barreling his way? And his great-aunt and grandmother behind him? The grandmother's name was Viv, if he remembered right, but he couldn't recall the great-aunt's name.

Axel's throat went dry, and he swallowed, the late August afternoon suddenly hotter than it was five seconds ago. *Let me be seeing things*, he thought. Correction: prayed.

"Danny, slow down!" one of the women called.

Prayer denied. That little boy in the dinosaur-covered T-shirt, blue shorts and orange light-up sneakers was definitely Danny Winston.

Axel's sister, the ranch's guest relations manager, had told him a family reunion was being held on the property, every bed in the six cabins filled, including cots brought in for the smaller kids. The clan was arriving today—and clearly had, given the crowd in the petting zoo. Had he asked their name? Probably not. Axel's job at the ranch revolved around guest safety and leading wilderness tours through the forest and up Clover Mountain. Knowing names and stocking the cabins with welcome baskets that catered to allergies and favorites was his sister's thing. Axel was more interested in sizing up guests' likelihood of getting lost and needing rescue; he kept watch over those types. There were lots of those. City slickers and country-bred alike.

"Zul!" Danny shouted as he came flying at Axel, twenty-five pounds of energy. The boy wrapped his arms around Axel's leg and squeezed.

Aw. Danny remembered his name. Well, half of it. "Hey there, partner," Axel said, scooping the tot up in his arms, the solid weight of him a reminder of three months ago.

"Hi, Zul!"

"Hey, Danny. Nice to see you again."

The boy beamed up at him with his bright white baby-teeth smile and those huge hazel-brown eyes. He was surprised Danny recognized him after three months, but maybe one of his relatives had pointed him out. *There's that nice man who rescued you from the mountain*, he could imagine one of the Winstons saying.

"Our hero!" called a woman's voice.

Axel glanced at Danny's grandmother as she approached. Her sister, Danny's great-aunt, was right behind her and holding a stuffed lion with what looked like a red cape.

"We hoped you'd be here!" the grandmother said. The Winstons had a strong family resemblance. Many were blond. The grandmother was tall and strong, her own ash-blond hair cut to her chin with a sweep of bangs. She extended her hand, and Axel shifted Danny so he could shake it. "I'm Viv, Sadie's mother. We decided to hold our family reunion on the Dawson Family Guest Ranch in your honor as a thank-you for finding our Danny."

The great-aunt stepped closer and extended her hand. "I'm Tabby Winston, Viv's sister."

As Axel shook her hand and smiled, he noticed Viv send her a scowl. He could feel the tension between the two women all around them. He wondered what that was about.

"I live here now," Axel explained. "Home was a cabin at the base of the Badger Mountain where I used to work, as you know, but I decided to move home—here—a few months ago. My brother, the foreman, and my sister, the guest relations manager, like having a search and rescue specialist on the property twenty-four/seven, and turns out I miss the cowboy life, so here I am."

That wasn't quite the whole story of why Axel had returned to the ranch he'd vowed to steer far clear of for the rest of his days. But then his brother Noah had become a dad—of twins—and his sister had a baby, too, and family tended to bring family around, didn't it? That wasn't the reason he was here either, but he liked the less messy versions of the truth. Poking around in his gut had never appealed to Axel. On mountains, in dangerous situations, when clocks were ticking, there wasn't much time for that kind of thing. Ranch life was a lot safer, and unfortunately, Axel had had a little too much time to think about a lot of things. Including his inability to stop thinking about Danny Winston's mother, Sadie. He glanced around the throngs of her relatives gathered around the barns, pointing at the alpacas and hoisting children to laugh at the goats' antics. He didn't see her.

"Zul!" Danny said, leaning toward his great-aunt and reaching out his hand.

"Here you go, sweets," the woman said, handing him the lion.

"Are we both named Zul?" Axel asked, unable to contain a grin.

"He turned his lion into Axel the Super Lion. Takes it everywhere," Viv said.

Danny flew the lion high and low. "Soup Zul!"

Axel felt a soft one-two punch land in his stomach, the effect that pure sweetness sometimes had on him when he didn't quite know how to digest it. "Well," he said, awkwardly leaning Danny toward his grandmother so he could transfer him to her.

Viv took him. "He's been saying your name ever since we told him we'd be going to the ranch where the hero who rescued him lives."

Hero. Axel hardly thought of himself as that. For a bunch of reasons.

A beautiful woman with long, light blond hair and pale brown eyes he'd never forgotten suddenly burst through a group of preteens. Sadie Winston.

"There you are, Danny!" Sadie said, taking a deep breath. "My little sprinter likes to take off and make his mother a nervous wreck. He'll keep you on your toes this week," she added to Axel, those eyes finally landing on him.

"Nice to see you again," he said. Quite the understatement. Seeing her again wasn't exactly nice.

The sight of her engendered all kinds of insane feelings he wasn't particularly interested in delving into. Her pretty hair caught the sun and held his attention for a second. She wore a white T-shirt, olive-colored pants and gray sneakers.

Out of the corner of his eye, he noticed her mother, Danny in her arms, moving over to where a bunch of chickens were pecking the ground. The great-aunt went to join another group by the alpacas' pen.

Just the two of them now. He had a sudden flash of putting his hands on Sadie's shaking shoulders, telling her he'd find her son. The look on her beautiful face, the absolute fear in her eyes. He wasn't returning to base a second time without the boy, and he hadn't.

He cleared his throat. "It was nice of your family to book the reunion here. Unnecessary, but nice."

"You're all my family has talked about the past three months. So trust me, it was necessary." Her smile lit up her face. "I hope saving Danny didn't put your job at risk," she added.

"It wasn't saving Danny that put my job at risk—it was me and 'my stubborn inability to follow protocol,' according to my boss. But it was for the best. It brought me home after a long absence and—" He stopped talking, realizing he was going off on tangents he had no interest talking about. *So why did you bring it up?* he wondered.

He'd broken some rules to find Danny, mostly concerning Axel's own safety because the sun had just set. His punishment was two weeks enforced R&R, which had been fine with him. He'd surprised himself by returning to the family guest ranch that he and his siblings had inherited when their father died almost a year ago. And he'd never left. He liked his job here, patrolling the vast property on horseback to make sure all was as it should be, guest-wise, ranch-wise. And boy, were there always a lot of kids at the ranch. His niece and nephews—three babies, two his brother Noah's and one his sister Daisy's, and then countless kids of all ages as guests. At first, Axel had been overwhelmed by all the kids, but then he'd settled into the sight of them, charged with their safety on hikes in the forest and the minimountain just a mile behind the ranch. He'd thought being responsible for them would do him in, but instead, it filled him up, gave him back a tiny piece of himself every time he stopped a kid from careening off a cliff.

"Oh, my!" a voice yelped above the fray.

Axel turned; a very elderly woman in a wheelchair was on the path in the main petting zoo, a white chicken on her lap. Fluffernutter. She liked human laps and loved being picked up and snuggled by kids. Most of the chickens accepted their hugs for the extra grain they knew would be coming their way. Any chickens that nipped a two-year-old's hand for daring to come too close were kept in a separate coop with a kid-free run.

"Declan," a younger woman shouted, "take the chicken off your great-great-auntie's lap this instant!"

"Sorry, Great-Great-Auntie," a boy with light brown hair said, scooping up the chicken and setting it down.

"Don't be sorry, Decky!" the elderly woman told him. "I asked him to put the chicken on my lap," she called out. "I miss having my own chickens."

The younger woman nodded at the boy, who put the chicken back on his great-great-aunt's lap. The smile on the elderly woman's face managed to warm Axel's heart.

"That's my great-grandmother, Izzy," Sadie said, her gaze on her relative. She turned to Axel. "She's ninety-nine years old. It was Izzy who started the tradition of annual family reunions. She used to hold them at her small ranch, but she lives with one of her daughters in town now, and no one has a property big enough to hold us all and keep the kids entertained."

"She looks happy to be here," Axel observed, the joy in Izzy's eyes clear from where he stood.

Sadie's mother returned with Danny, the boy still flying his superhero lion. "Axel, we'd like to invite you for a toast tonight at a bonfire by the river. Around eight o'clock? The young ones will need to get to bed soon after, so it'll be quick. Please say you'll come."

He glanced at Sadie, whose eyes had widened as though she'd had no idea such a thing would be happening. The knowledge he'd see her tonight was both very welcome and a problem he didn't want to think about too deeply. Something about her had gotten inside him in a way nothing had for three years. He'd recognized it right away— pure attraction, an inexplicable chemistry out of nowhere, an emotional pull. He'd tried to chalk it up to the situation on the mountain, the frayed nerves, the promise he'd made and would have died to keep. Anyway, Axel Dawson wasn't going back to that time three years ago when a single mother had torn his heart in two.

"Zul and Zul!" Danny gleefully shouted as he flew his lion around and then pointed to Axel.

Oh, man.

"Please come," Great-Aunt Tabby said, approaching them. Her sister, Sadie's mom, lifted her chin and turned away, the tension between the two women so thick Axel could bite it. "We owe you everything."

He was about to say he was just doing his job,

but finding lost people wasn't a "job." It never had been and never would be. Search and rescue was who he was, the call in his blood and veins. That simple and uncomplicated.

He looked at Sadie, who seemed to be biting her lip, her cheeks slightly pink. "Of course I'll come," he said, and the women beamed.

Well, except for Sadie. Something was up there, but again, he wasn't about to think about it.

The way he saw it, after one simple toast tonight, the hero stuff would be over. He'd stay fifteen minutes, shake some hands, smile at some kids and then he'd be free. The name of the game.

Chapter Two

"How ridiculous is this?" Sadie's sister, Evie, younger by three years, complained as she flopped on the twin-size bed in their cabin's bedroom. "Mom and Aunt Tabby haven't spoken, except to yell at each other, in *three* months!"

"Very," Sadie agreed, glancing at Danny, who was fast asleep in his porta-crib at the end of her own twin bed. She should be unpacking her and Danny's clothes and toiletries, but she just wanted to sit her butt down and think. And *not* think at the same time. That was how things had been lately.

For example, she both wanted to think and not

think about Axel Dawson. Everyone had been saying for three months that he was her hero, and damn right he was. But she had to keep her thoughts from running wayward, such as fantasizing about things that would never happen. One of her great-gram's favorite expressions was *You never know.* But Sadie did know because she'd overheard those rangers. She'd be completely delusional to hope that Axel would magically fall for her. Her family hadn't gotten the memo, though, despite her resending it countless times.

On the way from the petting zoo to the cabin, Sadie pushed her great-gram's wheelchair and looked for escape routes while her mom and grandmother pressed for details on what Sadie and Axel had been talking about in front of the barn. Had he asked for her number? Had he asked her out? Would they be riding horses into the sunset this afternoon? Three sets of Winston eyes had been full of hope.

Save me, she'd sent heavenward, but her nosy relatives kept at it.

"My, is he handsome," Great-Gram had said.

"That's some physique!" her grandmother had put in. "You know, he reminds me of—who's that handsome actor, Irish, I think? With the dark hair and blue eyes?"

Pierce Brosnan. And yes, Sadie totally saw it. Pierce back in the 007 days. Gorgeous. Like Axel.

"Look," Sadie had said. "I know you all want me married off, but Axel is not the guy for me. He's not interested in commitment. Do you want me falling for a guy who'll never propose?"

"Like your poor sister," Sadie's mother had whispered, turning and looking to make sure Evie wasn't in the vicinity. She was a few minutes behind them, walking with cousins, it had turned out. Sadie had wished her sister had walked to the cabin with them—she desperately needed her to change the conversation, and that would be easily accomplished, unfortunately, because of Evie's broken heart. Her relatives were all over that—the big breakup two nights ago on Evie's twenty-ninth birthday with the man she'd expected to propose. Sometimes the family was too much, like with Sadie, and sometimes they were heaven-sent, like when you were hurting so bad you couldn't stand up straight. The Winstons had rallied around Evie, keeping constant vigil, bringing her pints of Ben & Jerry's and boxes of Puffs tissues with aloe vera. The reunion would be good for Evie—a week of family support and long walks in the fields and petting alpacas.

Sadie hoped the week would have a similar good effect on her mother and aunt—who were not on speaking terms. They refused to talk about why, so no one could help the situation—and now the two were in separate cabins. Every year prior,

Sadie, her sister, mom, aunt, gram and great-gram all shared living quarters for the annual family reunion. Sadie's dad and grandfather were in cabin number three with Sadie's uncles and male cousins. Everyone was seriously relishing being among their "own species," as they called it, for an entire week.

One of the worst parts of the cold war between her mom and Aunt Tabby? That Sadie felt like it was her fault. The feud had started on the mountain when Danny had gone missing. Ugh. If only Sadie had been watching Danny more closely, she would have noticed he'd run off, and if he hadn't gotten lost, her mom and her aunt wouldn't be blaming themselves and each other—or at least, that was what she figured was at the heart of the fight. Things had been hunky-dory between them until that night.

"It feels so wrong that Aunt Tabby isn't staying with us," Evie said, pulling her shoulder-length blond hair into a low ponytail with a tiny velvet scrunchie from her toiletry bag.

It really did. There were two bedrooms in the roomy cabin, which could sleep six, enough for them all. Three in the larger bedroom, two—well, plus a porta-crib—in the smaller one and, if necessary, one person on the couch in the living room. Sadie's mom, gram and great-gram were sharing one room, Sadie, Danny and her sister in the other. This cabin was only one story, so both bedrooms were on the first floor, key for a ninety-nine-year-old great-gram, and for a mom needing to lug a stroller.

"I know," Sadie said. "I would gladly sleep on the couch and give my bed to Aunt Tabby, but she was adamant about sharing a cabin with her cousins and their families this year."

"Yeah, because she doesn't want to share a room with her sister," Evie said, popping up to unpack her suitcase into the closet and dresser. "What do you think happened between her and Mom? They got into an argument on the mountain when Danny was lost, right? I wish I'd been there so I'd know more. But nothing else makes sense. That's when it started."

Ugh. The elder Winston sisters had always been so close, thick as ole thieves, and now: narrowed eyes, scowls and sarcastic comments under the breath. "I think so, but neither will talk about it. And you know how getting either of them to change their minds about anything is." Both women were equally stubborn and always thought they were right. Sadie loved both women fiercely, but come on—get over it, already! This was the annual family reunion, and they should be celebrating being Winstons—not carrying on some grudge.

"Well, every time Mom asks me if I'm okay about the breakup," Evie said, practically strangling the gray yoga pants in her hands, "I'm going to ask her about her breakup with her sister. Maybe she'll stop asking!" Evie mashed the yoga pants into a ball and dunked them into the dresser drawer, then sighed and folded them nicely.

Sadie eyed her sister as Evie reached into her suitcase for her favorite hoodie, long, pale pink and fleece lined. Evie's face looked like it might crumple into crying any second, and Sadie's heart constricted.

Evie had given her boyfriend of three years an ultimatum two nights ago on, yes, her twenty-ninth birthday, and instead of getting down on one knee in the fancy restaurant he'd taken her to, which was what Sadie had expected all during dinner, he'd tearfully said he just wasn't ready. Evie had left the lovely peridot birthstone earrings he'd given her in their velvet box on the table, gulped the rest of her wine and left, sobbing all the way home. Sadie knew this because Evie had called her two minutes into her walk home, and Sadie had rushed over in her car to pick her up and bring her to her house, where her sister had cried in her arms for hours.

Evie had done similarly for Sadie almost three years ago when her then-husband had told a newly pregnant Sadie he wasn't cut out for fatherhood, sorry, and that he was leaving with the rodeo. They'd been married two months at that point, and according to her ex, marriage made him feel like he was stuck in quicksand. *Ouch* didn't begin to cover how bad that had hurt. She'd loved her husband, even if she knew they'd had some big problems that hadn't quite reared their ugly heads during the three months they'd dated prior to the backyard wedding at her grandparents' house. The divorce, taking all her dreams of a family with it, had devastated Sadie, and Danny's father had never come back, even to meet his son. These days, she was trying, at least, accepting fix-ups and blind dates and saying yes to coffee or dinner with the okay-seeming men she met while at work or around town. So far, she'd give her dating experience a D minus. Maybe even an F.

The Winston sisters both needed a heart boost—not their beloved mother and aunt in a big fight during what should be a soothing, if not fun week away with the whole family.

"Marshall hasn't texted!" Evie muttered, glancing at her silent phone on the dresser top. "Two days and nothing. Doesn't he even miss me? Three years and nothing?" She burst into tears and dropped on the bed, letting herself fall backward.

"Aw, I'm sure he misses you like crazy," Sadie said, going over to lie beside her sister. She took Evie's hand, both their gazes on the ceiling, which was a lovely post and beam, something she hadn't paid attention to when they'd arrived. The cabin was really nice—rustic yet spa-like at the same time. Sadie and Evie were both appreciators of spa-like.

"I want to marry him, Sadie. I want to have four children with him. I want to adopt an adorable shaggy dog from the Prairie City animal shelter. I want to start my future with the man I love more than anything on earth, except you guys. Instead, it's all over." Evie broke down in fresh sobs. "Why did I give him an ultimatum?" she croaked through her tears. "Why couldn't I just be okay with how things were? And things *were* fine. Even if we weren't planning our future."

"You asked for what you wanted and needed," Sadie pointed out gently. "That's the most important thing you can do. You were honest with yourself and him."

Evie swiped under her eyes and squeezed Sadie's hand. "Fat lot of good that did me. Honest and miserable. Thanks so much, universe."

Sadie couldn't help laughing, and suddenly Evie was laughing, too, then she sobered up and let out a sad sigh. A little noise and minigrunt came from the porta-crib, which meant Danny had woken from his nap. "Perfect timing, Evie. Let's go raid the cafeteria. I hear the cook makes incredible gooey desserts. There has to be something out now for hungry new arrivals." It was two thirty, and the cafeteria wouldn't open for full service until four thirty for dinner. However, Daisy, the nice guest relations manager, and Sara, the ranch forewoman, had greeted the family at check-in and said there were always goodies and refreshments on the tables near the door in the cafeteria and in the lodge beyond it.

"Good idea," Evie said, getting up.

If Sadie were being honest, she'd admit that she wouldn't mind clapping eyes on Axel Dawson again. She'd see him tonight, but there were hours to go. *Do not build some fantasy around him*, she warned herself. *He doesn't do commitment. You are looking for commitment. Do. Not. Go. There.*

There was falling ridiculously in love-lust with the man who'd changed her entire life, made happiness possible, made her future possible by finding her son when he'd been missing for hours. She owed Axel and his partner, that heroic Lab who would not leave that certain spot on the mountain, despite it seeming to lead to nowhere a toddler could get into, *everything*. Dude, the dog, knew his job, and Axel, the handler, knew his dog. Because of that, Danny had been found. They were *heroes*. No other word for it.

Which meant Sadie's inability to stop thinking about Axel was hero worship. *That's all it is. Toast the guy tonight and then emotionally move on.*

So easy to say. Doing so would be another story. Which was why she would not give her sister any dumb platitudes about broken hearts and time or changed minds or even her dear great-gram's *you never know*, though that one was true. Sadie would just listen and be there. But gooey desserts always helped, as did Danny's adorable ways, so Sadie got up, scooped her son out of the crib and let his huge hazel-brown eyes work their magic on Auntie Evie, who played five rounds of giggling peekaboo before they headed out of the room.

"The Winstons asked permission to make a bonfire by the river tonight," Axel heard his sister say, "so if you see big plumes of smoke in that direction, the cabins aren't burning down."

Axel looked up from where he sat at his kitchen table. Daisy Dawson, the ranch's guest relations manager, was outside on his porch, bent over with her face close to the screen. "Actually, I was invited to the bonfire," he said. "I'm practically the guest of honor."

She made an *ooh* face—Daisy loved being in the know—and seconds later she was in the kitchen, pouring herself a mug of coffee and joining him at the table. He was already on his second mug since returning from the petting zoo. He'd been going over notes he'd taken at the staff meeting this morning about the ages of the guests, safety issues, special requests—one woman used a wheelchair, one teenager had a broken wrist and another kid was deathly afraid of snakes and would scream at the top of his lungs if he saw one, garter or not, and go running blind, potentially off a cliff. Otherwise, the group members were in good general health, enjoyed light hikes and were used to the setting. Most weren't riders, so he'd have to be vigilant when they were on horseback. He and several of the ranch hands would constantly patrol the trails.

"Remember when I was sent home on enforced R&R after rescuing a kid on Badger Mountain back in May?" Axel asked.

Daisy sipped her coffee and nodded. "Of course I remember. It's what brought you home finally. I owe that rescue everything."

Axel smiled inwardly with a matching head shake. His sister had been trying to get her brothers to come home to the ranch they'd grown up on. The youngest Dawson sibling, Noah, had rebuilt the guest ranch their grandparents had started over fifty years ago, and he ran the entire operation, his wife the forewoman. Daisy had come back in the spring because Noah had needed help with a baby left on his doorstep, a crazy story that had turned into their brother becoming the proud married father of *twin* babies. Daisy had been pregnant then, and when her baby's father left her at the altar— literally—she'd ended up marrying the man who'd delivered her baby on the side of the road. That was also a crazy story.

Two Dawsons were married with children, happily settled into family life, and though Axel had made his sister's day by moving home permanently and building a cabin at the far edge of the property for himself and his trusty partner, Dude, the greatest dog there ever was, marriage was not in his plans. Daisy kept trying to fix him up, and he kept disappointing her. At least there were three other Dawson brothers out there she could work on. Rex, Zeke and Ford were scattered across Wyoming.

"Well, the family here for the reunion this week is *that* family," he explained. "Turns out they booked the ranch as some kind of thank-you."

Daisy gasped. "You're kidding! I wish they'd let me know. I would have put extra goodies in their welcome baskets or something."

Axel finished his coffee. "They keep calling me a hero. I'm only going to the bonfire tonight because they want to toast me. Then I'll leave."

Daisy grinned. "You are a hero, Axel. Accept it."

He wasn't. Heroes didn't let people down, and Axel had let people down plenty in his day, particularly the women who'd come and gone in his life over the past few years. But no one more than his own father a week before he'd died last December. Axel had found or rescued a lot of people in his days—years—on the search and rescue team. But he'd been a clueless idiot about his own father, who'd basically drank himself to death.

Daisy's phone pinged. "Duty calls," she said, popping up. "I'm meeting Sara at the river to set up the bonfire. Two of the hands will be on duty, too, so we should have a lot of eyes on the littles, especially."

He nodded. "I'll come help." He'd keep on his staff shirt, which would put some distance between him and the Winstons. He wasn't a guest who could hang out and chat; he was an employee of the ranch.

Dude came padding over, and Axel gave his buddy a vigorous pat and a kiss on his furry head.

"You stay here and take a nice nap, partner," Axel said to the dog. "Back in a couple of hours."

"Does he know what you're saying?" Daisy asked, looking from Dude to Axel.

Axel laughed. "Nope. He has a great vocabulary, natural to his former job as a search and rescue K-9, but not a string of chatty nonsense like that. He knows from the tone of my voice that it's all good."

"Maybe I can talk Harrison into adopting a dog. I want two pugs, one black, one fawn."

Axel raised an eyebrow. "Pugs? With the smushed-in faces?"

Daisy gave him a punch in the arm. "They're adorable!"

"I like big dogs, but yeah, I guess they are pretty

cute. Think Harrison will agree? He doesn't strike me as the dog type."

Daisy's husband was a businessman who'd originally come into their lives with some diabolical plan to steal the ranch out from under them. Ten years ago, long before their brother Noah had rebuilt the guest ranch, their dad had drunkenly signed over ownership to Harrison's father after losing a poker game. In the end, Harrison had let it all go and ended up with the real prize: Daisy. His sister might drive Axel nuts with her matchmaking and texts with attachments of articles about how married life improves heart health, but she and Noah were his best friends, and he was damned lucky to have gotten so close to the two of them and their spouses, for that matter.

He and Daisy left the kitchen through the arched burnished wood doorway that led to the living room with the vaulted wood ceiling and the stone fireplace, which right now had a huge basket of dried flowers in it, a housewarming gift from the ranch hands, which had touched him. He'd been living here for only six weeks, the house taking record-fast time to build, thanks to the team he'd hired to work beside him. He had to say, he loved this place. The cabin reminded him of the small one he'd left behind at Badger Mountain, but he'd added luxe, modern touches. Even Daisy, who wasn't a log cabin type, said she could happily live in his house. For a guy who'd planned to visit the guest ranch only when he absolutely had to, Axel Dawson had truly come home. His way, on his terms, which made it feel not just okay, but right. He felt like he belonged here.

But as he walked out with Daisy, he was well aware he had some unfinished business to take care of regarding being back: a letter he was avoiding and had since last December. His father had left each of his kids a letter with their name on it inside a folder marked My Will on his kitchen table. Axel's letter remained unopened under his socks in his dresser drawer. Eight months and counting. When Axel got low on socks, and the envelope appeared through them, he'd get an acidy pang in his chest and shut the drawer fast, reminding himself to do laundry.

Heroes weren't afraid of letters, and Axel would be the first to admit he was scared to know what was inside the one beneath his socks.

Daisy headed to the buggy she'd driven over in. It was a golf cart that Noah had rigged up to be ranch employee transportation across the vast property. They all had one, though Daisy's had yellow leaves painted on the sides. "You'd better take your own buggy," she said, "or you'll be trapped without a ride home since I'll be staying till the bonfire is over."

"Good idea," he said. His cabin was only five

miles from the area where the guest cabins were, and he could run that in twenty minutes, but would he want to after a long day and fifteen minutes of being thanked by Winstons? Probably not.

"See you there," he said, waving as he got in his own buggy.

As he drove, he was well aware that he couldn't get there fast enough. Because he wanted to be looking at Sadie Winston. He wanted to see Danny running around in his light-up sneakers. Maybe tonight would be a way to get them out of his head, out of his system.

Did that *ever* work, though?

Chapter Three

All thirty-eight Winstons had gathered on a rise near the river, mesmerized by the bonfire protected by a circle of rocks that the staff had set up. The children, and there were several, had been ordered under penalty of long time-outs or leaving early not to step past the rocks to get closer to the fire. Each kid had to agree, and only then had Daisy and Sara lit the bonfire.

From where the group sat on blankets, sipping soda or wine and snacking on various treats from little cream-filled chocolates to cheese and crackers to grapes, Sadie watched Axel Dawson walking the perimeter of the fire. He was just as mesmerizing as the flames. Could he *be* more attractive? Tall, over six feet, and leanly muscular with thick dark hair and features that were both refined and masculine at the same time. He wore the forest green Dawson Family Guest Ranch polo shirt and sexy jeans.

Sadie's attention was pulled from him by the clinking of a glass. She looked toward the sound to find her grandmother Vanessa two blankets over, tapping a fork against her wineglass. Her petite grandmother stood, her wavy gray-blond bob blowing in the breeze.

"Welcome, Winstons, to this year's family reunion!" Gram announced. Clapping, cheers and finger whistles followed. "We're here to have a wonderful time and relax and enjoy the guest ranch, but also to thank a very special person— Axel Dawson, the search and rescue specialist who found our Danny-boy when he was lost a few months ago during a family hike. Axel's family owns this ranch, and he now works here. I'd like to raise a toast to Mr. Dawson, our family hero! Everyone, raise your glass or sippy cup!"

Everyone leaped to their feet, the cheering and clapping deafening. Danny slept through all the hoopla.

Sadie looked over at Axel and could swear the

family hero was blushing, which made him more appealing, dammit.

"I had no idea he was so hot," Evie, sharing Sadie's blanket, whispered. "I mean, he's no Marshall Ackerman, but wow."

Sadie smiled and squeezed her sister's hand. Marshall Ackerman was the one who hadn't given in to the ultimatum. Sadie would describe him as attractive enough—he was a very smart tax accountant and a little buttoned-up, but Evie, who'd met him at her previous job—she'd recently become a CPA with a big firm—found him and his sweater-vests incredibly sexy.

"I know," Sadie whispered back. "It's distracting. But I refuse to let his hotness affect me—the man doesn't do commitment."

"That's going around," Evie said with a scowl. Then she raised her glass to toast. "Men—who needs 'em?"

"I'll clink to that," Sadie said on a grin, clinking her sister's wineglass.

As the family settled on the blankets and raised their glasses and cups and sippy cups to Axel, who looked like he might flee at any moment from the attention, Sadie held her own glass up, her gaze locking with his. He nodded at her, and she nodded back.

During the next ten minutes, Axel shook hands and hugged relatives and repeated the story of finding Danny. He gave credit to Dude, the ace yellow Lab with his excellent tracking skills, and held her family rapt. Sadie was now in a circle of relatives, including her sister and four of their cousins, near the fire, Danny still asleep in his stroller beside her. She listened to her cousin Wendy tell a funny story about the parent-teacher conference she went to last June, Sadie's attention more on watching Axel move from group to group. She hoped he wouldn't take off before they got a chance to talk again.

There you go again, she thought. *Wanting to get up close and personal with the anti-commitment one.*

"Excuse me," Daisy Dawson said as she approached their group. Sadie could see the Dawson family resemblance between Daisy and Axel—particularly the blue eyes. "I'm looking for Evie Winston."

"That's me," Evie said, turning from where she'd been chatting with two of their cousins.

"You have a visitor at the welcome gate," Daisy said. "A Marshall Ackerman? Shall I let him in?"

Evie gasped. "Marshall is here?" She turned to Sadie. "Marshall is here!" she repeated. "He's come to his senses!"

Sadie hoped so. The man wouldn't drive a half hour from Prairie City to return a jacket Evie had left at his place or her toothbrush, especially during a Winston family reunion.

"The gate is a quarter mile from here," Daisy said. "I'll walk you over and escort you both back."

"Thanks," Evie said. She turned and opened her eyes wide at Sadie, her expression so hopeful that Sadie sent up a little prayer that Marshall Ackerman had a diamond ring in his pocket. As Evie and Daisy disappeared around a curve, Sadie kneeled beside the stroller and gave her boy a kiss on the head. He was still fast asleep.

"Everything okay?" Axel asked, coming over, gesturing at the path toward the gate. "I saw my sister walking one of your relatives away."

"Everything's fine. That was my sister—Evie," Sadie explained, straightening. "Her ex-boyfriend turned up at the gate. Evie gave him an ultimatum at her birthday dinner—they'd been together three years—and instead of proposing, he said sorry. That was two days ago, but now he's here."

"To propose?" Axel asked.

"She hopes so," Sadie said. "And trust me, so does everyone else. My family is very marriage-minded."

He mock-shivered. "I'm not."

Yeah, she'd heard. But hearing it straight from him stung her anyway. "Why?" she asked. "If I can be so personal. I'm curious about what makes you know you don't want to get married."

He glanced away for a moment, then at her. "The very thought squeezes the air out of my lungs."

That sting she'd felt a second ago? Now a swarm of bees attacked as a memory of her ex-husband flashed into her mind. *I feel like I'm in quicksand, Sadie. Sorry, but that's how I feel. I thought I could do this, but I can't...*

"So marriage is like death?" she asked—coldly, she realized, but she couldn't help it. "A slow, suffocating death?"

He eyed her. "I wouldn't go that far. It's just not for me. I'm a lone wolf."

When someone tells you who they are, believe them...

She lifted her chin. "Well, I'm excited about the idea of finding my Mr. Right," she said, not that he asked. She took a second sip of her wine. She'd chug the entire glass if she were with her sister. "Love, partnership, sharing a life together. That's what it's all about."

He nodded. "I have a great dog."

She couldn't help laughing—not that that was funny. He seemed both serious about that dog comment and not. *You don't know because you don't know him. Keep it that way, missy—or you'll pay!*

Sadie had that funny feeling as if someone was watching her and turned to find her mother, grandmother and great-grandmother, plus her grandfather, two uncles and three cousins watching her talk to Axel. Her mom winked. Her grandmother raised a glass. Her great-grandmother was smiling and giving a little clap.

Oh, brother. If she had a bullhorn, she'd let them know what he'd said about marriage. *A slow, suffocating death, people!* She was paraphrasing, but she was right on the money.

Her grandmother pushed her own mother's wheelchair toward Sadie. The two looked so much alike, but Vanessa was twenty-six years younger. Ninety-nine-year-old Izzy's hair was a beautiful pure white that she always wore in a wispy bun, but she and her daughter both had colorful eyeglasses perched on their noses and hanging off beaded chains, purple for Vanessa and royal blue for Izzy. They both had the same warm, open faces and had never met a stranger. Sadie adored them both. "Izzy and I are pooped," Vanessa Winston said. "See y'all tomorrow for breakfast. I hear the cook makes the best chocolate chip pancakes in Wyoming."

Axel grinned and nodded. "It's true. The best everything. But Cowboy Joe's pancakes are divine. The other day, I had six, and we're not talking silver dollars."

Vanessa and Izzy chuckled, and from the absolute delight in their eyes, Sadie knew they were bursting with approval that she and Axel had been chatting away in their own little duo near the fire, Danny between them in the stroller.

"Night night, you two," Izzy said with a grin, adjusting her small square glasses. "Don't stay out too late."

Oh, brother. "We won't, Great-Gram," Sadie said. "Good night."

"I'd be happy to push the wheelchair and escort you to your cabin," Axel said, stepping over.

Both women beamed. "Oh no, dear," Vanessa said. "You stay and have a lovely evening with our Sadie. Did you know she won a blue ribbon at the county fair for her cinnamon strudel? She's quite the baker. And the loveliest gal inside and out."

Earth, please open and swallow me. Thanks.

"I do love cinnamon baked goods," Axel said with a nod—and a twinkle in his eye. Oh, God. So he had a good sense of humor. Or was he just kind to grandmothers and great-grandmothers? Sadie sighed inwardly.

"Hear that, Sadie-girl?" Vanessa said with a wink. Right there out in the open. No subtlety at all with this crew!

"Night, now," Izzy said as Vanessa waved and headed up the path.

"Good night," Axel called, watching them until they disappeared from view. He chuckled.

"Izzy, my great-grandmother, is ninety-nine."

Sadie wanted to head off anything about that last discussion. "Isn't that something?"

He smiled and nodded. "You're lucky. My grandparents and great-grandparents are all gone. As is my dad. My mother lives in Florida where it's always warm—she has a small orange grove."

Sadie had visited Florida once in the dead of winter and had never been more grateful for a state. "That sounds wonderful. Fresh-squeezed orange juice every morning." She bit her lip, suddenly feeling...shy-ish. "You've got lots of siblings, right? That must be nice."

"It is. There are six of us. Three of us live and work on the ranch. The other three are scattered across the state. They come home for occasions. Like the grand reopening of the ranch last Memorial Day weekend. And for Daisy's wedding—which didn't work out the first time around but she ended up giving birth that same day, so we were all here to welcome little Tony."

"So you have a baby nephew?" Sadie said. "How great for him to have two uncles right here."

He nodded. "I have another baby nephew and niece—twins. My brother Noah's kids. He runs the place, and his wife, Sara, is the forewoman. Turns out I'm better at babysitting than I thought. Chase and Annabel—Noah's twins—love me for some reason. Either that or I bore them to death with my stories about search and rescue, and they fall right asleep."

Sadie laughed. "So you like babies, but you're not planning on becoming a father yourself?" She immediately felt her cheeks burn. Why had she blurted that out? Ugh.

He glanced away again, something he did, she noticed, when he seemed uncomfortable.

He got lucky not having to answer because just then, Sadie could see Daisy Dawson, Evie and Marshall Ackerman heading toward them, and her attention went straight to her sister. Evie and Marshall were holding hands!

And as they got closer, Sadie could see a diamond ring glinting in the glow of the fire and the moonlight on Evie's formerly empty left hand. *Oh, Evie*, she thought, her heart overflowing with happiness for her sister.

Daisy headed over to where the ranch hands were keeping watch on the bonfire, and Evie and Marshall joined Sadie and Axel.

"I see congratulations are in order," Sadie gushed, blinking back tears as she took her sister's hand to see the ring. "It's so beautiful! I'm so happy for you two."

Evie wrapped Sadie in a hug. "I always love a good surprise. And this was the topper!"

Marshall smiled at his fiancée. "I was a fool— no, a complete idiot," he said, his dark brown eyes shining on Evie. "But two days on my own made me realize I can't live without this amazing person. Evie, you're the woman of my dreams. I'm sorry I made the last few days so painful."

"You are so forgiven," Evie said, grinning, reaching up to kiss him. "Oh! Marshall, this is Axel Dawson. He's the search and rescue specialist who found Danny when he went missing. This bonfire gathering is actually about a toast to him. And Axel, this is my brand-spankin'-new fiancé, Marshall Ackerman." She was positively beaming. "My fiancé. That will not get old."

Axel extended his hand and Marshall shook it. "Congrats."

Marshall smiled. "Thanks for saving my soon-to-be nephew. I'm crazy about this little tyke," he added, looking at Danny.

"Well, we've got to go share the big news," Evie said. "Mom is going to flip!"

Sadie watched her sister and Marshall tell her mom, who almost exploded with sheer joy. Hoots and hollers and cheers went out as word spread.

"Well," Axel said, "congrats on gaining a brother-in-law."

"Marshall's a great guy. I'm glad he realized what he'd be throwing away."

Axel stared at her for a second, and Sadie hoped he didn't think she was speaking code for herself! That was how much trouble she was actually in already with this man. Reading into absolutely nothing. Worrying about crazy nonsense. She had to get a hold of herself. Which meant heading to the cabin and getting away from those piercing blue eyes and incredible body—which was very close to her.

"Well," she said brightly, "time to transfer the big guy to bed." She smiled at the sleeping Danny. "To the porta-crib, anyway."

"I was about to head out, so I'll walk you then come back for my golf cart," he said.

Sigh.

"I'll push the stroller," he offered.

"Chivalrous. Your dad raised you right." She smiled, but the look on his face had her biting her lip. She stepped aside and he took the handles and they began walking up the path toward the cabins.

"Actually, my father destroyed everything he touched," Axel said, staring straight ahead. "He was a selfish alcoholic."

She stopped walking and so did he. "I'm sorry. That had to have been hard. Growing up that way."

He nodded and resumed walking. "My mother wised up to his cheating and finally left. We lived in town for years, and she thought it was important that we keep in close contact with our dad, so she'd drive his three boys over every other weekend. That's how I got so close to Daisy and Noah.

They have a different mother but were living here full-time in those days."

"So their mom—your stepmother—looked out for you and your brothers when you visited?" she asked.

"Yup. She was a kind woman, and she died way too young. After that, Rex and Zeke and I didn't come around too often since our mom didn't trust Bo Dawson with our lives even for a weekend. Our oldest brother, Ford, also has a different mother, and he refused to visit at all once he got old enough to protest."

"Did your dad have any redeeming qualities?" Sadie asked, hoping so.

"I suppose everyone does. He was a charmer. Always had nice girlfriends who deserved a lot better. He cared about us in his own way, I guess. Sometimes he shocked me with the undeniable truth that he loved us. But he was a wrecking ball of a man. He destroyed the guest ranch his parents built. He destroyed his marriages. He disappointed his kids constantly. He hurt everyone he came into contact with."

"Is it hard being here, then?" she asked. "You've only been living here a couple months, right?"

He nodded. "It was hard at first. But there's a lot else here. My grandparents' legacy—even if the ranch is a lot different now than the one they began. Family history. Memories—bad but good, too. My dad had absolutely nothing when he died—cirrhosis of the liver from years of drinking—but he left us all this ranch, which at the time was abandoned and a wreck. And letters. We each got a personal letter."

"Did yours help?"

He shrugged. "I still haven't opened it."

She gaped at him. "Really? Aren't you curious?"

"Yes. Very. Always have been since I got it last December. But I can't bring myself to open it."

Huh.

"Well, here you are," he said quickly as though suddenly aware he'd said too much or at least much more than he'd intended on a two-minute walk.

Sadie glanced up at the cute dark wood cabin with its white trim and barn-red door. There were blooming flower boxes in the windows and two white padded rocking chairs on the covered porch. Sadie's grandmother was sitting in one of the rockers, a glass of iced tea and cookies beside her. Izzy's wheelchair was parked beside the little ramp on the side of the porch. Izzy could get around fine on her own, particularly with her cane, but she always used the wheelchair for crowded areas or distances. "How nice of you to walk Sadie home," Vanessa said with a big smile.

Sadie pursed her lips. "Gram, guess what? Evie

got engaged! Marshall came tonight and proposed. They're still at the bonfire sharing the big news."

"What?" Gram flew down the steps and wrapped Sadie in a big hug, her floral perfume, her trademark that Sadie had always loved, enveloping her. "That's wonderful!"

"What's so wonderful?" Izzy asked, coming out on the porch in her flowered ankle-length bathrobe, using her bright red wooden cane with its copper handle.

"They're engaged! Oh, I'm beside myself!" Vanessa said, completely overcome. "I'm going to make a few happy calls to let people know— back in a bit!"

Gram had been one of Evie's biggest ralliers when Marshall had broken her heart, buying her an as-seen-on-TV zip-up blanket with pockets that she'd stuffed with packets of tissues and packs of M&M's and gummy bears, Evie's favorites. Sadie had no doubt Vanessa would go through the list of her besties—her bridge club, knitting circle and ethnic cooking class.

As Gram hurried inside, Izzy settled on one of the rockers, stealing a cookie. "Engaged! Oh, happy day!" Her eyes misted, and she patted her chest. "Well, come up and let me congratulate you two! Oh, how wonderful indeed. My Sadie, engaged!"

Sadie glanced at Axel. Izzy couldn't possibly

think she and Axel were the engaged ones. "Uh, no, Great-Gram, it's—"

"I'll tell you, Sadie-girl," Izzy interrupted. "When that louse of a husband up and left you pregnant and alone, I cried myself to sleep for weeks. All I've wanted in this world is for you to be happy. And now that I'm nearing the end of my days, I'll know my girl has found everlasting love with a real hero. You two have made an old woman so happy," she said, looking from her to Axel. Tears ran down Izzy's wrinkled cheeks.

Oh no. No, no, no. "Great-Gram, I—"

Axel leaned closer. "You can correct her in the morning—or Vanessa will when Izzy heads inside to bed. She's probably tired right now and extraemotional."

Sadie nodded. Extraemotional was an understatement.

"Well, come now, give your great-gram a hug," Izzy said, holding her arms out wide.

Sadie went up the steps and bent to hug Izzy.

"I haven't been this happy since your great-granddaddy was still with us," Izzy whispered, wrapping both hands around Sadie's face. "I love you so much, Sadie. You deserve this happiness. And you," she said with utter reverence, turning to Axel, "our family hero. That precious little boy in that stroller will finally have a daddy, and a wonderful one at that." Tears shone in her hazel eyes.

"Come hug your great-gram. You can call me that or Izzy, whatever you like."

Axel smiled tightly, leaned over and gave his new great-gram a hug.

"If I go into that good night, and I just might, I'll go happy now," Izzy said, a hand to her heart again.

Sadie felt her eyes widen to the point they ached. She glanced at Axel, who looked equally shell-shocked.

"Well, um, good night, Izzy," Axel said, clearly forcing a smile.

"Didn't I tell you to call me Great-Gram? We're family now!"

Sadie bit her lip. Izzy could get a bit addled now and again. This would be easy to correct in the morning when Izzy had had a good night's sleep.

"See you tomorrow, Great-Gram," Axel croaked out. He glanced at Sadie, then at Danny, and then ran for the hills.

Sadie's heart was beating a mile a minute. Oh, God. This was a mess.

Gram would help straighten things out in the morning. Vanessa would simply tell Izzy that *They're engaged!* referred to Evie and Marshall, which made complete sense, and not Sadie and Axel.

"I'm zonked," Izzy said, slowly getting up with the help of her cane.

"Let me go put Danny in his crib, and then I'll be right back." She parked the stroller by Izzy's wheelchair, then rushed inside with Danny in her arms, hoping to catch Vanessa between calls, but when she poked her head in her gram's room, Vanessa was chatting away on the phone about hoping to find the grandmother-of-the-bride dress of her dreams.

Sadie hurried into her room and settled Danny in the porta-crib with barely a stir out of him, then went outside. She helped Izzy into the cabin and to the bedroom she was sharing with her daughter and granddaughter. Vanessa was still on her cell phone, talking excitedly. She lowered her voice when Sadie got Izzy into bed, Great-Gram closing her eyes and snoring within seconds. Today had been a big day for everyone—arriving at the ranch, the orientation and walk around the property, the bonfire and the big news, which was not news at all—but especially for the ninety-nine-year-old.

As Vanessa sat on her bed, telling whomever she was talking to that no, she had no idea if Evie would take Marshall's last name or keep her own, Sadie knew her gram would be on the phone for at least an hour more. She managed a smile at Vanessa and waved, then slipped into her own room.

For tonight, until morning, Sadie was engaged to Axel Dawson. And that was fine with her.

Chapter Four

Axel yawned early the next morning as he towel-dried his hair and ran his hands through it, then pulled on his Dawson Family Guest Ranch staff shirt and a pair of jeans. He'd slept like crud, waking up constantly as though he'd forgotten something important. And then he'd remember: he was fake-engaged for the night. To Sadie Winston. Even being faux-engaged had unsettled him to the point he couldn't sleep. All that talk of a hero for a husband and a wonderful father for Danny.

Eh, it would all be taken care of by now. Izzy's daughter or granddaughter or great-granddaughter had probably set her straight at some point last night. Marshall Ackerman was the only groom-to-be in the vicinity.

It was barely 6:00 a.m., and the sun was dawning a hazy pink over the horizon, but there was a lot to prepare for today—wilderness hikes and trail rides and river swimming, plus some general cowboy duties to help out his sister-in-law, Sara, the forewoman. Axel went to grab a pair of socks from his dresser drawer, and there it was. The letter.

He really should move it somewhere he wouldn't notice it so often. Through the low jumble of rolled-up socks he could see the *Ax* of his father's scrawl on the front of the white letter-sized envelope. Knowledge of his illness had prompted his father to write the letters, but not to talk to his children. What was in there? *Sorry for being a terrible father 98 percent of the time?* That was what Axel figured. Noah and Daisy and Ford had all shared their letters. Noah's had been full of apologies and asked him to think about rebuilding the ranch that Bo had let rot. Noah had surprised all the siblings by stepping up and meeting the challenge, and they'd all invested in the Dawson Family Guest Ranch 2.0. Daisy's letter had also apologized for letting down his only daughter time and again but he'd left her her mother's wedding rings, which Daisy had asked for since she was eleven, when their mother had died. A broke drunk with a gambling problem, Bo could have sold the rings for a decent amount, but he'd held on to them, knowing how much they meant to his daughter. Axel had always thought Bo had hung on to the rings instead of giving them to Daisy so that he'd have something over her, something she wanted from him, to keep her from completely turning her back, which she wouldn't have done anyway.

Axel had. And then his father had died a week later.

He shook that away and thought about Ford, the oldest of the siblings, who'd tried the hardest of all of them to get through to their dad. Even Ford, a cop who'd seen just about everything, had finally had enough. Ford's letter from Bo hadn't been a letter at all but a map, a hand-drawn rendering of where he'd buried Ford's mother's diary, which Bo Dawson had found one day, apparently not appreciated and hidden somewhere on the property in a drunken stupor. Apparently, Bo figured Ford might want to know his mother's secrets, and so he'd left him the map, just a map, no note, nothing. Ford had tried to find it a couple of times since he had known the general area, but hadn't been able to.

As for Zeke and Rex, neither would say a word about their letters. Rex was private, always had been, to the point that no one knew what he did for a living. Axel was pretty sure he worked for the government, either local or federal, in some secret-spy sense. For all Axel knew, though, Rex could be a lobsterman out on a boat all day. The man just would not say. Zeke was a successful businessman a few hours away and had done a lot, remotely, to help Noah in getting the ranch up and going operationally. But on the rare occasions the six siblings were together, every time Daisy brought up the letters their father had left them, Zeke changed the subject or suddenly had to make a call.

Axel grabbed the letter and held it up to the light as he'd done a thousand times. He wouldn't mind making out a few words or a sentence to get the general gist. He could make out the dark scrawl of his dad's handwriting but not individual words. He put the letter in the drawer. He wanted to know what it said—and didn't. The story of his life.

He sure had been chatty last night on the way back from the bonfire about his father, though. What was that about? Why had he said so much? All those deeply personal details about Bo Dawson's issues. Maybe Sadie was easy to talk to. They'd shared a very intense…something on Badger Mountain when Danny had been lost, when he'd promised her he'd find her son. There was a connection there. That was all. So he'd opened up. Not something he ever did, though, so the fact that he had meant something. He just didn't know what.

He grabbed socks and shut the drawer, then

headed downstairs with Dude for much-needed coffee. He'd let the dog out in the yard and had barely had a sip before he heard his sister's sing-song voice out on the porch.

"So I hear congratulations are in order and that I must be so overjoyed to be gaining a sister-in-law," Daisy said.

Axel glanced through the kitchen window. Daisy, her face full of what Axel could call only about-to-burst-out-laughing merriment, peered at him through the screen.

What she'd said hadn't quite registered. Congratulations? A sister-in-law? What?

"Now, I know you, Axel, and there's no way you're engaged, so what the peacock is going on?"

Wait. If Daisy was being congratulated about the "engagement," that meant it had gotten around. But how was that possible?

"A great-gram, that's what," Axel said on a long sigh. He'd been sure the whole thing would have blown over by now, that someone would have explained to Izzy that he and Sadie weren't the engaged ones. If not last night, then this morning.

Daisy, dressed as he was in the Dawson Family Guest Ranch green polo but with khaki shorts, her long light brown hair in a braid, was in his kitchen like a shot, pouring herself a mug of coffee and taking a slice of banana bread while she was at it. "Okay, spill it."

He explained.

"Ooh, boy," she said. "Well, at least ten Winstons congratulated me this morning on becoming part of the family, Axel, and it wasn't even six a.m. You can thank sunrise yoga for so many guests being out and about that early."

He stared at her, horror building in his gut. "I don't get it. Sadie was going to tell her grandmother that Izzy had misunderstood her and they'd tell the great-grandmother—she's ninety-nine, by the way—together."

"Well, it doesn't look like anyone spoke up. So you're engaged." Daisy let out a hearty chuckle. "In fact, a Winston kid who couldn't be older than six came up to me and said she heard that my brother was marrying her big cousin Sadie and now we're all going to be one big family."

Axel gulped.

Daisy laughed. "I'm happy for you, Axel. It's almost like a dream come true, if it were real."

Axel groaned and slugged the rest of his coffee. "Keyword if, and it's not. We'll get it straightened out this morning." He stole a piece of banana bread.

"Speak of the bride," Daisy said, tipping her chin toward the window.

Axel looked out. A ranch hand was driving a golf cart toward his cabin, Sadie in the passenger seat.

"My cue to scram," Daisy said. "I'll do a lot of

smiling and nodding and hasty retreating around the Winstons until you say otherwise."

He groaned. "What a mess."

"An interesting mess, though," Daisy said with a grin, then left.

Axel let Dude in, then stood on the porch, watching Sadie hop out of the buggy and thank the ranch hand, who turned and drove off, following Daisy toward the ranch.

Sadie held up a hand in something of a wave, and he did, too. She looked kind of...stressed. Damn, she was pretty. Her long blond hair was loose and swaying a bit as she walked, catching the early sun. She wore a pale yellow tank top, white shorts and sneakers. A delicate gold necklace with a tiny letter *D* dangling glinted on her breastbone. *D* for Danny, he figured.

"I hear we're still engaged," he said as she approached the steps. "Little relatives of yours are congratulating my sister."

She closed her eyes and buried her face in her hands for a moment, then shook her head and looked at him. "I have made one heck of a mess of this."

"Come on in for coffee. I have bagels, or I could make you scrambled eggs."

Her face brightened—likely because he wasn't furious and screeching his head off about the whole thing. He had a feeling that was what she expected. Normally the idea of anyone thinking he was engaged would bring about that feeling he'd described to her last night: a lack of air in his lungs. But he was oddly calm about it. Maybe because he'd been there when the misunderstanding had occurred.

"I'd love a bagel," she said. "And about ten cups of coffee."

Yeah, me, too, he thought, offering her a smile. "Follow me. Dude's hungry, too."

He led the way into the cabin and she stopped to pet the appreciative yellow Lab and look around, slowly swiveling. "This is some cabin. Not what I expected," she added.

"What did you expect? More rustic?"

"Yes. This place is gorgeous. Such craftsmanship. And so cozy."

He felt a bit of pride as she slowly turned and took it all in, the woodwork and moldings, the furnishings. "I knew I needed to make this place my sanctuary to be really comfortable here. So I did."

She glanced at him, then settled her gaze on a watercolor of abstract sheep. "Makes sense, based on what you said last night. About your dad."

He swallowed. Yup, he'd said all that. He sighed inwardly and headed to the kitchen, so aware of her behind him. Dude followed for his own breakfast.

He fed his dog, then poured Sadie a cup of coffee and gestured for her to sit at the table. "Cream, sugar right here," he added, pointing. "So for bagels I have plain, sesame, cinnamon raisin and everything."

"Sesame with cream cheese would be great."

"I'd almost prefer to keep talking about anything other than the fact that your entire family thinks we're engaged," he said, cutting two sesame bagels and putting the halves in the toaster oven.

"Me, too," she said.

He smiled and sat, drinking the rest of his coffee. "Okay, I'm a bit more fortified now. Fill me in."

She took in a breath and blew it out. "Well, last night, I helped Izzy to bed, and she conked out right away. I'd planned to tell Vanessa what happened, that Izzy thought she'd been referring to us when she'd said, 'They're engaged,' but every time I went to talk to Vanessa, she was still on the phone. I guess I fell asleep because when I woke up at the crack of dawn, everyone was awake and talking about the possibility of a double wedding— my sister, mother, gram and great-gram. My sister was jumping up and down about my sudden whirlwind engagement. My mother was *crying*— seriously, tears streaming down her cheeks to the point she couldn't even speak. My grandmother was on the phone to let everyone know *both* her granddaughters had gotten engaged last night, and I was in total shock. Meanwhile, Danny started screaming his head off, so I took care of him, and when I came back, everyone was knee-deep in making lists of caterers and bridal boutiques and possible venues."

Axel smiled and shook his head. "Having met all these people, I can easily see how that all unfolded."

"I appreciate that. My family can definitely be overwhelming." She took a long sip of her coffee. "And then, I was about to tell them it was all a big misunderstanding when my aunt Tabby burst in and wrapped me in big hug, then my sister, and said she was overjoyed and that for the sake of the two brides-to-be, she hoped she and my mother could put aside their differences for the time being at least. My mother agreed to the truce, and I was so flabbergasted that I still didn't pipe up. It's been three months since their big fight, and two engaged nieces are simply bigger than their fight. I watched them talk—smiling and happy—for the first time since that day on the mountain, Axel. About wedding stuff, not themselves or actually making up, but talking."

He nodded and got up to take the bagels from the toaster oven and slather them with cream cheese. "Well, hopefully, they'll return to being sisters and put whatever happened between them behind them." She looked so eager that he realized her mother and aunt's cold war had been really tough on her, especially because he knew she thought it had something to do with Danny going missing that day. He added a small bunch of grapes to the plates, then brought breakfast over to the table and sat across from her.

She smiled and popped a grape into her mouth. "Thank you," she said, then bit into the bagel, sitting back and relaxing. He felt like jumping up and massaging the tension out of her shoulders. The urge to touch her was way too strong. "So then the lot of them were all excitedly talking again," Sadie went on, "and relatives burst in the cabin to congratulate me and Evie as they heard the news, and now I'm expected to go preliminary gown shopping this afternoon." She dropped her head into her palm, then looked up at him.

"They must have asked where your diamond ring is?" he said, eyeing her empty left hand.

"They sure did. I told them I decided I didn't want a ring this time around, that what mattered to me was our marriage and the wedding ring."

He nodded, not wanting to delve into that. "So where did you tell them you were going this morning?" he asked.

"To see my fiancé before his work starts," she said sheepishly, her cheeks bright red.

He smiled, but then the word *fiancé* reverberated in his head and that airless feeling started in his chest. "They're watching Danny?"

She nodded. "I'm so sorry about all this, Axel. Look, I'll text my sister right now and explain what happened, and she'll set everyone straight. It's embarrassing as heck, but by the time I get back to the cabin, they'll have forgotten it. There's still an engaged Winston sister. My mom and aunt can still find joy and common ground in that, and it'll help bring them together."

He was about to nod until he noticed how sad her eyes looked, how stressed she seemed.

He heard ninety-nine-year-old Izzy's voice from last night. *When that louse of a husband up and left you pregnant and alone...*

He'd always known Sadie was a single mother; he'd known that up on Badger Mountain when the team had questioned her and her family about the possibility of an unhappy ex snatching Danny when no one was looking. She'd said her ex-husband hadn't showed a lick of interest in the fact that he had a child, and she highly doubted he'd been following them and hiding behind trees, waiting for a moment to suddenly kidnap Danny and raise a son on his own. The louse had left her when she'd been seven weeks pregnant and hadn't been heard from since. She'd sent the divorce papers to his parents, and they'd sent the signed set back. Her ex had apparently said Danny wasn't his, and they believed him. A single mother completely on her own—that couldn't be easy, big family around her or not.

"I'll text Evie right now," she added, pulling her phone out of her pocket. "She announced that she and Marshall decided to have the wedding right here at the ranch at the lodge on the last night of the reunion, so everyone will be all excited about that. Evie also said she thought each of us should have her own big day, so that stopped the double-wedding talk." Her eyes misted, and she looked away, clearly embarrassed.

She *wanted* to be engaged, he realized, both superficially and deep down. Even faux-engaged—he understood that with sudden crystal clarity. All that happy attention, all that affirmation, her relatives stopping with the "poor Sadie, all alone" crud. His scruffy, scuffed-up heart went out to her.

Axel put his hand on hers to stop her from texting her sister. "I have an idea."

She peered up at him with those beautiful pale brown eyes.

He slugged his coffee, then looked at her. "I totally get what happened, Sadie. I've been in the middle of that kind of family melee where you're so overwhelmed by everyone's voices that you're speechless even if they're talking about you."

She stared at him with what seemed like utter relief that he understood. "But now we're engaged. What are we going to do? We have to tell them the truth. I mean, it's not like I can let them think I'm getting married when I'm not."

He took another bite of his bagel. "Here's the idea part… Your sister is getting married the last night of the reunion. Let's get through that, everyone focused on Evie and on her wedding, and once you're all home, you can tell them it didn't work out and you didn't want to say anything because you didn't want to take away from Evie's special day."

She stared at him again, her mouth slightly open. "You're serious."

He shrugged. "Why not? That way, a ninety-nine-year-old remains happy. Your mother and aunt will mend their issues."

"Wait. You're willing to be fake-engaged for a week for the greater good?" She gaped at him, head tilted.

And because something is telling me you need this, Sadie. Something is poking and pushing at me deep down, making that very clear. A flash of her face on Badger Mountain, when she'd been terrified, over an hour into her then twenty-four-month-old son missing settled in his mind. In his chest. In his gut. All the questions the police had subjected her and her family to. Was she a good mother? Was she neglectful? Did Danny often run off unattended? There were questions that had to be asked in that kind of situation, a complete picture drawn. But hell, she'd been terrified about her son. Now, she was on vacation with thirty-eight of her relatives, which couldn't be all sunshine and roses even in the closest of families. Yeah, he'd cut her a big break. Why not?

"I'm speechless, Axel Dawson. Well, actually, no, I'm not. You really are a hero."

He smiled. "Wait till you get to know your fiancé," he said. "You'll see I'm not."

She tilted her head again, her expression shifting, and he could have slugged himself. Why did he blurt things out with this woman? Why did he say what was in his head? Why couldn't he stay hard to talk to the way he usually was? Hadn't that been the complaint of 75 percent of the women he'd dated the past few years?

"All I know is that you've saved my life twice now," Sadie said. "And made me breakfast." Her smile lit up her face, and the sun glinted on her *D* necklace.

There was that urge to touch her again, to run his hand along her bare shoulders, to feel her silky blond ponytail. A realization slammed into him. He most certainly could not touch her. Not when they were fake-engaged. Because there was one thing Axel knew always got him into trouble, and that was a blurred line.

Chapter Five

This was nuts. Sadie had gotten through breakfast (Cowboy Joe's chocolate chip pancakes really were something spectacular) and a family walk on the wooded trails by the river, but now she, her sister, mom and aunt were about to leave for Your Special Day, a bridal boutique in Prairie City, which was a half hour away. Gram would be watching Danny and taking him to the petting zoo and then to the lodge for the "kid fun zone," where an indoor obstacle course, games and arts-and-crafts station, broken into age groups and run by the ranch staff would let tired grown-ups take a breather for a couple of hours.

Sadie sat on her bed in the cabin, her stomach churning. Her sister was standing before the dresser mirror, putting her hair in a ponytail and dabbing on lip balm that smelled like vanilla. Sadie stared at Evie, her best friend, someone she'd always been able to talk to about anything. Suddenly Sadie was lying to her about something so vital? No—Sadie wouldn't do this. She had to come clean. The sooner, the better. The longer she kept up this lie, the harder it would be to explain.

"I wasn't going to say this," Evie said, turning to face Sadie. "Because it sounds kind of 'poor Sadie,' which I know you hate. Which *I* hate. But one of the reasons why I waited so long to tell Marshall to fish or cut bait was because I hated the idea of getting engaged while you were...still single."

Sadie felt her cheeks flame, and she coughed. Oh, God. This was awful.

Evie sat beside her. "I love you to death, Sadie. You've been my best friend since the day I was born. I have no idea what I'd do without you— for advice, for sharing my every thought and secret, for analyzing Mom and Dad over the years... everything. But when that jerk left when you were pregnant... For the past two years, you've gone from my amazing older sister to more—you're *my* hero, Sadie. You've handled single motherhood like an absolute champ. You're so strong, so independent and such a great mom. But I know how badly that rat bastard hurt you. And there was no way I wanted to get engaged and celebrate all things love and forever when my favorite person in the world was on her own with a baby. Am I making sense?"

Tears streamed down Sadie's face. She had no idea if part of her was crying for the mess she'd made of this lie or all her sister had just said, how moved Sadie was by how much Evie cared about her.

Evie's eyes filled with tears, too. "Something in me came to a head with Marshall on my birthday, though. I realized that his not proposing after three years when we had something so special and good and right was like a slap in the face. Like, my sister didn't go through everything she went through so that you, Marshall Jay Ackerman, could be so lackadaisical about making a real commitment to me."

"I think I know what you mean," Sadie said, swiping a hand under her eyes. "You wanted him to put up or shut up because commitment matters, and you saw how little it meant to Danny's father even when a pregnancy came into the picture."

"That's it, exactly. And now, I'm engaged, and so are you! I can't tell you what that means to me. That you're happy, that you found your guy—and such a great guy—and that we get to do this together. All the fun bridal stuff."

Sadie wrapped her sister in a hug. So much for setting the record straight. *Oh, um, er, Evie? It turns out I'm not engaged and this was all a misunderstanding. Great-Gram mistook me for the bride-to-be and it snowballed and now you poured out your heart and soul to me, but oopsies—I'm still "Single Sadie" and my supposed fiancé and I haven't so much as held hands, let alone kissed.*

Yes, dammit. Just tell her the truth! It'll be mortifying for an hour or two and you'll both be embarrassed but you have to come clean! Of course, things will feel weird and Evie will feel awful that she'd said all that, and you'll create problems between you two when Mom and Aunt Tabby are mending their *fences, and today's shopping trip will be ruined for Evie.*

Oh flipperty-flubs. If Sadie didn't blurt out the truth right now, there would be no turning back and she'd have to go with Axel's generous idea to keep up the ruse for the week and let Evie have her week of happy engagement without anything mucking it up. As the truth would.

Speak now or forever hold your—

"Ready, girls?" their mom called from the living room.

Evie's smile was so big, so happy, that Sadie sucked in a fast breath and called out, "Yes, we're ready."

Well.

* * *

The moment Aunt Tabby parked her SUV in the public lot in the middle of Prairie City's two-mile-long downtown, Sadie wished she were at the Dawson Family Guest Ranch in Bear Ridge. Sadie had spent her whole life in Prairie City and the big town had a lot to offer, from the vibrant village with shops and restaurants to open spaces. The lot abutted the town green, which had a gazebo and a playground and picnic tables, and it was on a bench beside a bronze sculpture of Hazel Mont-vale, the town's intrepid female founder, that Sadie had told her then-husband, Kyle Harlow, that they were going to be parents.

She'd chosen the bench for two reasons—one, she loved that statue of Hazel and often, when she couldn't figure something out, she'd think: What would Hazel Montvale do? And Sadie would do the smart thing instead of the dumb thing. Two, the bench was right behind a low fence that sur-rounded the playground, and she liked the idea of talking about starting their family in the midst of toddlers and little kids on the slides and structures.

Her husband of two months had changed after the wedding. She'd asked her family to be honest about that—had it been Sadie who'd fallen for a scoundrel and dismissed all the bright red flags or had he truly changed? Her mother, honest to a fault, had said that Kyle had changed, that the gold band and the piece of paper had some triggering effect on him, though neither knew from what. He'd gone quiet, then stopped coming home after work, then stopped coming home before midnight and then some nights, didn't come home at all. Pleading for conversation, the truth, answers got her nowhere. And then she'd discovered she was seven weeks pregnant.

When she'd asked him to meet her at the bench on the green, she wasn't sure he'd show up, but he had because it turned out he had news, too. He'd made a mistake, he was sorry, he wasn't cut out for marriage, he loved her, but he couldn't stop wanting to sleep with other women, too. While he'd been talking, her head and her heart had been so numb she almost didn't bother telling him her news. But he should know, so she did and his response was not unexpected. *Sorry. Leaving with the rodeo. Tell the baby he or she is better off without me, that y'all can do way better.*

He'd left her sitting there, and if it were not for the statue of Hazel Montvale to the right of her, she would have fallen to a heap on the ground, unable to sit upright. Sadie had called her sister, who'd rushed over, and Evie had called Sadie in sick to work for the next three days with a bad case of strep throat. Sadie had cried her eyes out—for the lost dreams, for her baby who'd grow up without his father, for being thirty and pregnant and alone with a wedding band that now symbolized nothing.

That he'd gone from warm and funny and soulful to miserable, cheating and gone had done a number on her for a long time. Her ability to trust her own judgment had been destroyed. A few months after Danny was born, Sadie started agreeing to fix-ups and blind dates since her relatives were full of "he'd be perfect for you" lists, but no one was. No one had come close. A few times someone had seemed like a possible second date, but then he'd say something that would indicate he had no interest in becoming anyone's stepdaddy, let alone a loving father.

"Now, Sadie," her mom said, slipping her arm through her daughter's as they walked toward the bridal boutique with Aunt Tabby and Evie right behind them, "just because you had the big white dress and fancy reception the first time doesn't mean you can't have a bigger, splashier wedding this time around. With the *right* groom."

Sadie had always appreciated her mother's *go big or go home* mentality. But she swallowed. "I think the second time around, small and private sound perfect."

Viv Winston gasped. "Sadie Anne Winston, don't you dare think of eloping!"

"Ooh, you're thinking of eloping?" Evie called from behind them.

Sadie turned back. "Just thinking aloud. I don't know what I want yet."

"How about Axel?" Aunt Tabby asked. "He has a big family and probably wants the big wedding."

Sadie couldn't help but notice her mother stiffen beside her when Tabby spoke, Viv's expression tightening, too. Hmm. They might have declared a truce for the sake of Sadie and Evie being engaged, but they were clearly still in the same old fight.

"We haven't talked about that at all," Sadie said fast. "Things happened really quickly."

"I'll say," her mother added, tucking a swatch of her shoulder-length blond hair behind her ear. "I can't believe you two were dating right under our noses the past three months!"

Sadie *wished* they'd been dating. "I, uh, didn't want to jinx it. Whenever I talk too much about what's going on in my relationship, it's always doomed."

"Well, then don't say another word!" Aunt Tabby called out. "We love Axel!"

Her mother lifted her chin. "Even a broken clock is right twice a day," she whispered.

Sadie gasped. "Mom!" Good Godfrey, things between Viv and Tabby were way worse than she realized, given that they were both here.

Her mother gave an embittered shrug and hurried along. Your Special Day was two stores up.

"Mom," she whispered. "Please tell me what's going on between you two. What happened?"

Viv and Tabby—Tabby was four years younger—had always been so close. Aunt Tabby was more than just a beloved aunt—she'd never married and Tabby's house had always felt like an extension of Sadie's own or like a sanctuary to run to when she was angry at her parents or arguing with Evie about something dumb. Aunt Tabby had never wanted children, and often over the years, Sadie had heard overly personal conversations about the subject, sometimes including Tabby and sometimes not. None of the family, except Great-Gram Izzy, seemed to be able to comprehend a woman not wanting to have a baby and raise a family.

Oh, please! Izzy had said. *First of all, some kids turn their parents' hair gray by the time they're five years old. Who needs to spend their lives in a hair salon to turn back time when it's marching forward? And motherhood is not the be-all and end-all of a woman's life. There's her work and volunteering and friendships and bridge partners.*

Everyone had started in about Izzy having a zillion people to care for her in her old age because she had had children, but Izzy had harrumphed and said, *Oh, please, that was what great-granddaughters and grandnieces were for.* It was no surprise that Aunt Tabby worshipped her grandmother. Sadie had always hoped she'd inherited even just a little of Izzy's wisdom.

"Between who two?" her mother now asked.

Sadie made a face. "C'mon. You and Aunt Tabby."

"Everything's fine," she lied way too smoothly. "Oh, look, we're here!"

Sadie glanced at the beautiful window display of Your Special Day. A dress straight out of her dreams was in the window. She shook her head at herself. Why was she letting a wedding gown, which she would never wear because she was *not* engaged, distract her from her mother?

"Mom, please talk to me straight," Sadie whispered as her sister and aunt caught up.

"Ooh, look at those shoes!" Viv gushed, pointing.

"I love them," Evie said, coming up beside Sadie. "Peep-toe 1940s glam. I'm trying them on!"

Sadie glanced at her aunt, who was looking anywhere but at her own sister. She knew she wouldn't get any answers out of these two right now.

Sadie headed into the shop, the mannequins with their gowns and busts of headpieces and veils and jewelry reminding her of the first time she'd come here with these three women. Her grandmother had also joined them. "Let's make this week all about Evie's wedding," she said. *Please all agree that's a great idea and lay off me!*

"Well, take pics of anything that catches your eye for yourself," Aunt Tabby said. "I can help you make a mood board for your wedding."

"I found my dress!" Evie said, her eyes wide on a mannequin by the shoe display.

They all turned to look in the direction Evie's misty eyes were staring.

"Oh, Evie, that is so you," their mom agreed.

"Love it," Aunt Tabby said.

Sadie smiled at the strapless, white satin gown with delicate beading at the waist. It was like the peep-toe shoes her sister had admired: 1940s movie star elegance. As the saleswoman came over, Sadie found her gaze drawn to another dress, one that almost took her breath. She'd worn the traditional big white gown for her first wedding, but this one, tea length and ivory, had a vintage look to it. There was something a little "second wedding" about it, in a good way. Sadie imagined herself wearing that dress, Axel beside her in a bolo tie and Stetson and dark suit, a horse or the pair of alpacas behind them.

Snap out of it! she yelled at herself like she was Olympia Dukakis in *Moonstruck. Axel is never going to be your groom, and from the way your dating life has been going, you're going to be single a long time.*

Thing was, she really didn't want to be. Sadie wanted her life's mate, her love, her future, her family. And the more she looked at the dress and pretty veils, the more heart-pokingly clear it was how much she wanted all this for real. Not the *stuff*—but the love. The partnership. The life sharing. A father for Danny.

Axel Dawson was not that man. Hero or not, Sadie barely knew the guy, even if she felt like she'd known him forever. He'd told her straight out how he felt about marriage. So really, she should put her fantasies aside this week, not that she figured that would be easy or even possible.

Once the reunion was over and Evie was off on her honeymoon, Sadie would focus on what she really wanted and maybe join an online dating site where she could pick her own possibilities and weed out the no-ways and get to know a few guys via email and the phone prior to meeting. According to Aunt Tabby, who lived by her mood boards, you had to create the life you wanted. And if Sadie wanted love and commitment, she'd need to go find it.

Yes, Axel would be hard to live up to; the man was a real-life hero and intensely good-looking with incredible shoulders and narrow hips and—

"Ooh, my treat, Sadie-girl," her mother said, wiggling her eyebrows as she beelined for a display of sexy bras and matching undies, lace and satin and plunging. "Axel won't know what hit him."

Sadie was long used to her mom being right out there with her and Evie's sex lives in addition to everything else. She eyed the lingerie, wondering what kissing Axel would be like. Hot, very hot, no doubt. Wasn't she supposed to be shelving her fantasies about him?

"The black set is so sexy!" her mother gushed.

It certainly was. But when would Axel Dawson ever see her in the scraps of black lace and satin?

"I'll take two sets of these," her mother said, putting the bras and matching undies on the counter. "Evie will love them, too."

Before Sadie could make some excuse to put one set back, a gasp from Aunt Tabby had them turning around, and there was Evie, in her dress and veil and peep-toe shoes. The three of them were speechless, a rare occasion.

"Oh, Evie," Sadie whispered, hand on her heart. "That is definitely the dress."

Tears ran down her sister's face. She was definitely overwhelmed.

Her mother and her aunt Tabby hugged. Actually hugged each other! They seemed to realize they were caught up in an emotional moment and stepped back, each retreating with the expressions they reserved for each other these days, but they'd hugged. A good start. This week of wedding prep, the four of them spending time together over such a happy occasion, would do wonders for the elder pair of sisters.

"I'm saying yes to the dress," Evie said, her eyes misty and her face full of wonder. "And the shoes. And the veil." She bit her lip. "I'm tingling from head to toe."

Sadie eyed the lingerie on the counter and wanted more than ever to hang her set right back up. Evie's face, those tears, that dress—this was how it was supposed to be. Breathtakingly *real*. Faking this engagement, despite the reasons, felt so wrong again.

Her phone pinged with a text and she fished her phone from her purse. Axel Dawson.

Hope you're surviving this afternoon, he'd texted, adding a smiley face emoji wearing a cowboy hat.

Oh, God. The man was thinking about her. Caring about what she was going through. And let her know.

What hit her heart at that moment was very, very real indeed.

Ping! Another text from Axel.

Saw your grandmother with Danny at the petting zoo. Danny was flying his superhero lion over the chickens and promising Zul would save them from a "scawy monster." He's too cute.

Against all reason, Sadie Winston fell headlong in love.

* * *

Yes, a grown man was hiding. Axel Dawson was suffering from an acute case of being asked too many questions and getting too many hugs from strangers who were related to Sadie in some way. He glanced out the round window at the far end of the big barn away from where the horse stables started—yup, there were stray Winstons out there, looking over the horses from their half-open stalls. At least the equipment area of the big barn was shielded from view.

He was so focused on catching his breath from being too much the center of attention for even a minute that he hadn't heard his brother Noah come in until he heard him returning a rake to a supply closet. Tall, dark-haired and blue-eyed like himself, his youngest sibling looked a lot Axel, though they had different mothers.

"Ah, Axel, just the man I was looking for," Noah said. "Any reason why the guests are congratulating me on becoming an honorary Winston?" He pulled something out of the small messenger bag across his torso and held up a T-shirt that read Team Winston. "Your *fiancée's* grandmother gave it to me."

Axel grimaced as Noah smirked at him, holding the navy T-shirt with orange letters up to his chest. "I was hoping Daisy would have explained so I wouldn't have to. It's crazy enough to know it without having to say it all over again."

"Wait. You're actually engaged?" He eyed Axel. "Nah, there's no way."

"Of course I'm not," he said, touched at how well his brother knew him. Noah was the one who'd rebuilt the Dawson Family Guest Ranch from absolutely nothing. This barn had been a falling-down mess, one wall caved in from where their father had crashed into it with his truck last fall. Luckily, the buggy Bo had often driven around the property hadn't done too much damage when he'd ended up smashed into ranch outbuildings. How the man had survived all that was beyond Axel.

Only to be gotten by excessive drinking. Liver damage. He shivered despite the warm eighty-degree temperature.

Axel whispered the explanation—just in case big Winston ears were listening on the other side of the window. "So it's just for the week," he added. "A ninety-nine-year-old is happy. A formerly dueling mother and aunt are now on a bridal boutique shopping trip. Sadie's been through enough—I can do this for her."

Noah nodded slowly. "I knew there was a heart in there," he said, slapping a hand against Axel's chest.

"Let me ask you a question *and* change the subject," Axel said. "Did you open your letter from Dad right away?" Bo Dawson had died last December. It was now late August and Axel's unopened letter was still burning a hole in his sock drawer. Almost nine months had to be some record for ignoring a bequeathal.

Why was this on his mind so much now? Ever since he'd blurted out his life story to Sadie on the walk to her cabin last night, he couldn't stop thinking about the letter.

"Are you kidding?" Noah said. "I was afraid to touch it. Forget opening it. I kept expecting it to burst into flames or something."

Phew. So Axel wasn't crazy.

"But you did open it," Axel said. "Clearly. Because in the letter, Dad wrote that he thought you should rebuild the ranch, and you did that."

"Took me three days to open the envelope. Probably would have taken months otherwise, but curiosity got me. And Daisy kept calling me and asking if I'd read it yet. Like every half hour. I had no choice, man."

Axel laughed. "Yeah, our sister has a way of making things happen."

Three days for Noah, who was the curious type, was the equivalent of almost nine months for Axel, who'd always been more apt to *ignore* than act.

That idiotic trait and bad habit was pretty much the reason Axel was fake-engaged to a woman he'd spent about ten or so total minutes with three months ago. He'd thought he could avoid and deflect the Winstons this week by hiding in barns and behind buildings, but the family had been after him all morning, peppering him with questions about himself and his own family, their kind, open faces truly showing deep interest in him as a person—and future member of their clan. If only he'd insisted that Sadie come clean, rip off the ole Band-Aid in one painful tear. The truth would have put everything back to normal.

Maybe. Or maybe the truth would make everyone uncomfortable during a family reunion. He could practically hear them coming at Sadie, disapproval tingeing their voices: *Why didn't you correct Izzy in the moment? Why didn't you say something first thing the next morning? Why'd you pretend to be engaged during the bridal shopping trip?* Then faces would register understanding, and it would be *Poor Sadie. She probably wanted to be engaged like her younger sister so bad she didn't want to explain the misunderstanding.*

The one thing Axel did know for sure in this world was that when he opened that letter from his father, he'd have to deal with whatever was in it. Just like he was having to deal with being hugged and congratulated and told not to elope to Vegas, that just because it was a second wedding for Sadie didn't mean the whole family didn't want to watch her walk down the aisle to a real hero.

Actually, we're not really engaged, he'd wanted to scream about five times today. *Ninety-nine-year-old Izzy misunderstood and no one corrected her or anyone when word spread like wildfire.*

In fact, he was the one who'd told Sadie to let it go, to *not* correct, to let the "engagement" stand for this and that reason. Yeah, yeah, he was doing Sadie a favor and keeping the peace in her family, but was that all that had been about? Axel felt like there was something else poking at part of him deep down, demanding his attention.

Ugh. Like he wanted to analyze himself? That was his sister's job and she was annoyingly good at it. Maybe he'd go visit his baby nephew Tony and see what Daisy had to say about the why and what of his brain.

"Yoo-hoo!" called out a woman's voice. "Axel? You around here somewhere?"

Axel's eyes widened and he stared at his brother in horror. "Save me," he whispered.

Noah laughed. "He's in the big barn," the traitor called. "We'll be right out, ma'am."

"Well, aren't you a dear," whoever it was called back.

Noah smiled. "Your in-laws are calling. Shall we?"

"I'll get you," Axel said, shaking his head at his brother.

Outside, Noah lifted his hat at Sadie's grand-mother and great-grandmother and headed to-ward the petting zoo, which had a good crowd. The Winston clan sure loved those animals. They spent more time petting the goats and marveling at the alpacas and miniature pigs than they did at any other activity, such as riding or hiking.

"Oh, good, we found you," Vanessa said. "Someone said they thought they saw you head into the red barn. Axel, with all of us right here at the ranch, I can see you and Sadie aren't getting any time to yourselves, so Izzy and I thought the two of you would like to go into Bear Ridge for dinner and a movie. Just get away for a bit. You tell Sadie we'll watch our precious grandbaby."

Dinner and a movie?

"You go ahead and let her know right now," Izzy said with a nod. "Oh, she'll be so glad to have a night out on the town. Our Sadie-girl works so hard and then takes care of that little one on her own, then is always seeing to what we need. She deserves a night out away from all the hoopla."

Both women, with eyes so much like Sadie's, stared at him. And stared some more.

Axel pulled out his phone. "I'll, uh, text her."

Your gram and great-gram think you deserve a night out away from "all the hoopla." Dinner?—A

"What's he doing?" Izzy asked Vanessa.

"Texting," Vanessa told her mother. "Remember, it's like a letter over the phone."

"Like email?" Izzy asked.

"But faster," Vanessa said.

"So fast she already responded," Axel said, swallowing. "Her answer was Yes, please."

The women beamed. "Have a wonderful time, Axel."

As he watched Vanessa push Izzy's wheelchair, two girls with blond braids coming flying at them and talking excitedly about the miniature pigs, he wondered just what had happened to his life.

Chapter Six

Almost like a real date but not, Sadie thought as she eyed herself in the mirror above the bureau in her cabin's bedroom. Based on Axel's text, he'd obviously been ambushed by Vanessa and Izzy. He'd probably felt cornered into texting her about the date right then and there. But Sadie *could* use a night away from her family—despite the fact that the reunion had barely gotten underway. Plus, she and Axel could figure out how exactly they were going to pass as engaged when they'd never spent any time together. Though, of course, her gram and great-gram had fixed that tonight.

"You're not wearing that, are you?" her mother asked from the doorway, her arms crossed over her chest with a tsk-tsk expression. "You're going out on the town with your husband-to-be! Doll up a little!"

Inward sigh.

"I think your yellow sundress would be perfect for tonight," Viv added with a firm nod.

Sadie glanced at her pink T-shirt and her favorite jeans, soft and worn. "Bear Ridge is a casual town, Mom." She *was* planning to change, not into a dress, though.

Sadie had brought two dresses for just-in-case situations while at the dude ranch, but even the more casual sundress was too much for tonight. "I'm going with the white jeans and the floaty blue-and-white peasant top Evie gave me for Christmas last year. I love that blouse."

"Fine," her mother conceded. "But with those cute metallic wedge sandals—not sneakers!" Viv added. "A little makeup would be nice, too."

Viv Winston would definitely win any Pushy Mother of the Year award. But maybe Sadie could glam up a little. At the ranch, she just put on sunscreen and lip balm, but she *was* going out to dinner. Even if her grandmother and great-grandmother had commandeered her "fiancé" into it. Sadie really did want to get out of Dodge—for a few hours.

"Don't forget a light dab of perfume," her mom said as she stood and headed for the bureau. "I'll take the tags off the new bra and undies—"

Okay, there was a line and her mother had crossed it. Sadie's cheeks were hot—either from embarrassment or disappointment that no, she would not be wearing the sexy bra and underwear tonight. Even if she wanted to lead her "fiancé" to bed, this was *way* too soon. Sadie had left her things on the shelf at Your Special Day, but apparently her mother had bought it along with Evie's.

"I'll save those for the honeymoon," Sadie said, about to tell Viv to leave her be before Sadie lost her mind.

Thankfully, her mother's phone pinged with a text and Viv skedaddled to meet four of her cousins for smoothies and sunset yoga at the lodge.

Sadie put on some makeup, gave herself a once-over and had to admit she did look like she was going on a date. *Oh, what the hey*, she thought and dabbed her favorite perfume on her wrist and behind her ear.

She headed through the quiet cabin onto the porch to await Axel. Vanessa and Izzy, babysitting Danny, were with a big group of relatives on a sunset river walk, and her sister was actually in Prairie City for the night since she was having dinner with the Ackermans and staying over at their house tonight. Sadie breathed in the quiet, random voices and laughter and crickets in the background. She could hear a car coming, and her heart sped up.

A navy SUV pulled up beside the cabin and there was Axel in dark gray pants and a button-down shirt, rolled at the forearms. Seemed he got the memo about tonight, too.

He opened the passenger door, which got the evening off to a very date-like start. When he got in, she was too aware of him so close to her. He smelled delicious.

"Have a craving for any type of food in particular?" he asked.

"Hmm, I could go for Mexican. Enchiladas or sizzling fajitas, maybe. And a margarita. I really need one of those."

"Me, too," he said with a smile. "Mexican it is. There's a place right in town that I've always heard was good or we could go to Prairie City— I think there are two Mexican restaurants there."

"I'd love to try the Bear Ridge one since I've never been. But you haven't either?"

"It was one of my dad's hangouts so I tend to avoid it, but he always raved about the food. Let's give it a try."

"If you're sure," she said, trying to give him an out. Based on what he'd told her about his father, she wasn't sure he'd want to be reminded of the man. But as she sneaked a glance at him, his expression was tension free as he started the car and drove off. "So, my grandmother and great-gram cornered you, did they?"

He laughed. "Izzy is very persuasive."

"That she is. I think the generations got even pushier. Well, except for my generation. Evie and I are pretty mellow."

"Glad to hear that, fiancée," he said, shooting her a grin. His face lit up and so did her heart. "I figured a night to ourselves would give us a chance to talk through how we're supposed to act around your family."

"So your brother and sister know the truth?" she asked. "I figured they did—just want to double-check. Your siblings haven't welcomed me to the family."

"Yup, they know the whole story. They'll nod and smile and be vague, particularly Daisy, whose entire job is dealing with guests."

The moment Axel drove past the open gates of the Dawson Family Guest Ranch, waving at a young woman in the forest green "Welcome" shed, Sadie felt herself relax. They were headed into a Winston-free zone, no talk of weddings and wedding night lingerie. Sadie could catch her breath.

Fifteen minutes later, they'd arrived in the center of Bear Ridge, a small town with a teeny village center. There was an old-timey general store that also served as the post office, plus a library, town hall, various businesses like a law office and nursing home, and a few restaurants. Manuela's Mexican Café was colorful and illuminated with many hanging lanterns. There were tables out front, separated from the street by a row of planters full of flowers.

"Inside or out?" Axel asked as they approached the restaurant.

"I think in," she said. "I'd like to be in the midst of all that fun ambience."

He smiled and opened the door. The restaurant was low lit and more romantic than Sadie realized it would be, the lanterns casting soft glows all around. Paintings and Mexican artifacts covered the walls, and a huge cactus was by the hostess's station.

"Evening," the hostess said. She wore a sleeveless red velvet dress, a ton of necklaces and bracelets and killer black patent heels. Her long silver hair was the only giveaway that she was in her sixties. "Table for two?"

"Yes, please," Axel said.

The woman peered more closely at him and gasped. "Now, I know that Bo Dawson, God rest his soul, passed on last year, but my goodness, you're his spitting image. One of his kids?"

Axel gaped at the woman. "Axel Dawson," he said, extending his hand.

The hostess clasped his with both of hers. "Manuela Gomez," she said with a smile. "Owner, hostess and keeper of history. And yup, I knew it! Bo Dawson was a regular here for years—thirty years from the week we opened. I'll never forget the first time he came in because he fell madly in love with his waitress and came in twice a day every day during her shifts until she agreed to go out with him. Her name was Diana."

Surprise lit his eyes. "Diana is my mother's name," he said, and Sadie got the feeling he wanted the woman to keep talking *and* to go away. "Could it be her? I didn't know she worked here."

"Definitely her because she married him a few months later and they went on to have three children, all boys, and you are one of three, no? I think he was divorced with a young son at the time."

Ford, Axel's eldest brother, Sadie realized. Axel didn't respond to that, which made Sadie wonder if Bo Dawson *had* been divorced at the time. Then again, if he'd married Diana after just a few months of meeting, he likely had been.

"Diana was putting herself through college when they met," Manuela said. "Her old clunker of a car always broke down and so he gave her his truck so she could safely get to work and school. He would walk the five miles from his ranch here to sit in her station and have tacos just to see her because she was so busy. And he never showed up without either flowers or candy. Your mom was a jelly bean addict."

From the look on his face, Axel definitely didn't know about any of that either. "Still is," he said.

Manuela smiled. "I guess it didn't work out between them in the long run since I know he remarried after some years and had two more kids, but while your parents were dating, I remember thinking, now that is a man in love."

Axel smiled tightly.

"Well, here I am rehashing old times and you two are probably starving!" Manuela said, grabbing two menus. "Come, let me give you one of my favorite tables." She led them to a roomy square table for two by the ornate fireplace that was festooned with tall glowing white candles inside the hearth. She looked up and snapped her fingers, and a waiter immediately appeared. "You take good care of these two," she told the young man.

After they ordered—margaritas, frozen, no salt for Sadie and straight up for Axel, steak fajitas for her and enchiladas *suizas* for him—the waiter quickly returned with their drinks and a basket of homemade tortilla chips and three kinds of salsa.

"First," Sadie said, raising her glass, "a toast to escaping the craziness."

"I'll definitely drink to that," he said, clinking his glass with hers.

"So was all that Manuela had to say a surprise to you?"

He set his drink on the table and swiped a tortilla chip through the salsa *verde*. "I knew that my mother put herself through school as a waitress but not that she worked here. I definitely didn't know any of the other stuff Manuela mentioned."

"Sounds like your father was madly in love with your mom."

"In the beginning, sure. He probably swept her off her feet with his grand gestures of giving up his truck and walking five miles to see her with jelly beans. And then time ticks on and they're married with three little boys, and is he home? No. He's probably here, drinking at the bar and falling in love with another waitress and bringing her Kit Kats."

Yikes. "It doesn't help to know he had a compassionate, loving side, despite all his faults?"

Axel took another sip of his margarita. "Help? Not at all. In fact, it makes it harder. If Bo Dawson had been more of a complete one hundred percent jerk, I would know what to do with my—" He stopped talking and grabbed a chip.

"Your...feelings about him?" Sadie attempted.

He glanced at her, his blue eyes a mix of emotions. "Yeah. Sometimes it's easier for things to be more black-and-white. You can close a door that way. Yes, he was a serial cheater and alcoholic who left my mom with three kids under six and unsteady child support *and* a man who'd walked ten miles there and back to see her because he'd given her his truck so she'd have reliable transportation to work and school."

"I like that part," Sadie said.

"Me, too. But Bo was also famous in the family for passing out drunk on the porch, needing his young boys and their visiting older brother to help pull him in the house. Sometimes we couldn't budge him and just had to cover him with comforters. Toward the end, he was crashing into the barns in the buggy or his truck. He wouldn't listen to anyone." For a moment he seemed to be lost in a memory.

"Oh, Axel, that sounds rough," Sadie said, her heart constricting for the kid he was.

He sipped his margarita and glanced out the window, then back at her. "Then there's a memory that always comes to me when I'm thinking about my dad at his worst. A good memory."

Sadie wasn't surprised there was one and probably many.

"When I was a kid and my grandparents were still alive," he said, "we had this Dawson Family Guest Ranch tradition that every time they brought home a new animal, one of us kids got to name it. The day it was my turn, my grandparents brought home a black goat with gray horns and I named it Flash. I was crazy about him. At the time, I considered him my best friend."

"Aw," Sadie said, biting a chip. She could see him sharing his troubles and hopes with Flash the goat.

"One day, Flash took off at night and got lost up on Clover Mountain. I was so upset, trying not to cry and failing. So many wild animals lived up there and I thought for sure Flash would be eaten within hours. Well, my dad took me out to look for Flash, and when we found him trapped on a ledge but had no way to call for help—this was before cell phones and my dad had lost his radio—we hunkered down because he knew I couldn't bear to leave Flash there. Finally, well after midnight, a search party came and Flash lived a good long life."

"It's clear he did care about you, Axel," Sadie said.

The waiter arrived with a tray of their food, and Axel seemed relieved for a reprieve from the highly personal conversation.

"Your family seems close," he said, cutting into his enchiladas.

She smiled, heaping steak and vegetables onto the flour tortillas. The food smelled so good she could barely wait to take a bite. "We are. Sometimes they drive me nuts, but I know how lucky I am. My mom is super pushy, but I'll tell ya, when you need your mama, there's no one you'd want more than Viv Winston at your side. Sometimes I think all that fierce family love ruined me for relationships."

"Wait, what?" he asked, his fork paused midair.

"Maybe I expect too much. Want too much. Think the man I'm seeing will treat me the way my family does and then be disappointed when a guy forgets something important I mentioned during the last date or doesn't consider my feelings."

"Sadie. There's no such thing as expecting too much. The man in your life *should* love you fiercely."

"That's what I want," she managed to say but the conversation was all too much. She'd said too much. "For me and Danny."

He looked up then, his blue eyes locking with hers, then got busy eating.

They clearly both needed a break from how personal this had gotten.

"So things are better between your mom and your aunt?" he asked.

"Not really. They're doing things together for the sake of me and Evie, but I hear the under-the-breath snipes and see the looks."

"What do you think started it? You said it had to do with something on the mountain the day Danny went missing?"

"I think they both blamed each other. Danny was walking with them, behind me and my cousin Daphne, and then he was gone. But they won't say why they blame each other. I can't see how they can. They were both walking with him and watching after him as he toddled along. He was only twenty-four months then."

"Think this week will help repair the relationship?" he asked.

"I hope so. When I see them like this, it makes me realize this could happen between me and Evie—and she's my best friend. Just like Mom and Tabby were best friends. I hate to think of anything coming between *us* for months."

When the waiter appeared to clear their plates, Sadie hadn't realized they'd finished practically every bite. Moments later, he appeared with two desserts on the house, thanks to Manuela. Sadie was stuffed but she couldn't resist a sopaipilla with its cinnamon sugar and a bite or three of the cheesecake flan.

Conversation during dessert and two cups of coffee each had turned to their favorite desserts and then favorites in general. Sadie discovered that Axel was a french fry addict and could eat turkey and provolone sandwiches on French bread every day for lunch and pretty much did. He loved Marvel and DC movies and Westerns. He liked the color orange. His favorite season was summer, same as Sadie's.

I want to kiss you, she thought as he reminisced about Flash the goat, his favorite childhood pet.

After goodbyes and hugs to Manuela, they were back in his SUV. Sadie was again so aware of him so close beside her that she started rambling. "So who's your favorite superhero?" she asked. "Let me guess. Iron Man. No, Captain America."

"Neither," he said with a smile, turning toward her. "My favorite superhero is Zul, the flying lion."

Before she could stop herself, she reached a hand to his face, too touched to speak, and he leaned over just slightly and kissed her gently on her lips. Mmm. She kissed him back and suddenly their hands were everywhere, hers on his rock-hard chest, wishing she could undo some buttons and feel his bare skin, his hands on her neck, in her hair. He was definitely her favorite kisser. That was for sure.

Even the thought of marriage makes me feel like the air is squeezing out of me.

Oh foo. This kiss had to end. Now. She couldn't get carried away with Axel "Marriage Is Suffocation" Dawson.

She pulled back. "As much as I want to keep doing that, you heard me say tonight that I'm looking for someone to love me and my son fiercely. You're not that guy."

He stared at her but didn't say anything. She'd rather have a firm *You're right, I'm not* than his silence. She'd actually prefer a *You're so wrong, I'm already crazy about you so let's forget the past and start anew with how we feel right now.*

But he didn't say that either, of course. He just

covered her hand with his for a second to say he understood and then nodded and started the SUV.

Axel liked how forthright Sadie was. He'd liked kissing her even more. They'd gone out tonight to escape her family's closing in on them, and instead, he walked right into *his* family's closing in on him. Between Manuela's stories and everything he'd said at dinner, Axel had felt off-kilter as they'd gotten into the SUV to head to the ranch.

And he was including that lighthearted dessert conversation of their favorites. He'd been charmed and amused and touched by Sadie and the stories about her favorites. Butter pecan was her favorite flavor of ice cream because she'd tried it for the first time the day before her great-grandpa had passed away and it always reminded her of how sweet and loving he'd been. She loved romantic comedies and tearjerkers, and had seen the movie *9 to 5* with her favorite singer, Dolly Parton, at least twenty-five times and credited it for making her laugh through her divorce.

She loved Pink Lady apples and the color teal and being near bodies of water, whether the ocean or a pond. And her favorite person, her very favorite of all favorite people, was her son, Danny.

His head and chest and every part of him had been so full of Sadie Winston by the time they'd gotten from the restaurant into his car that he'd been dying to kiss her. When she'd touched him, put her hand to his face, he couldn't resist the overwhelming urge, and as he leaned toward her, she leaned toward him, and whammo. A kiss that had exploded in his head.

Then it ended all too soon. But Sadie was right. She was looking for something real. And he was Status Quo Axel and liking it that way. Needing it that way. His head was in a good place right now and he wasn't about to muck that up when it had taken so long to get here.

Sadie's phone pinged, and she fished it out of her purse.

He caught her expression change as she read it. "Everything okay?"

"Actually, no. My mom says that Vanessa and Izzy are both sneezing and coughing up a storm. She thinks we should get Danny and stay at your house for a couple of days till they're not contagious. She'll take care of them, she says."

Wait. Sadie and Danny—in his house? Staying with him? For a couple of days?

"I'm sure we can stay in the lodge, right?" Sadie asked. "I'll text Daisy."

"There aren't guest rooms in the lodge. Just the couches in the main room. Of course you two will stay with me. We have extra buggies, so I'll borrow one for you so you can get back and forth to the action as you want."

She bit her lip and stared at her phone screen. Then she looked out the window. "I don't know, Axel. Things got kinda hot and heavy before. How are we going to share your house for an hour, let alone a day or two?"

"I won't let my lips get anywhere near yours," he said. He held up two fingers. "Scout's honor. And you know I was an Eagle Scout."

She tilted her head. "Your dad helped with that accomplishment?"

"Actually, a time or two when he was around and alert. My oldest brother helped the most. I'd call Ford and he'd ask his mom to drive him over for a couple of hours."

"That's really nice," she said. She bit her lip again. "Well, if you're sure you don't mind having us at your home. Danny wakes up early. And sometimes he still wakes up during the night."

"No problem," he said.

Or was it?

Chapter Seven

They'd stopped at Sadie's cabin to pick up her and Danny's suitcases—which her mother had already packed so that Sadie and Axel wouldn't have to come in and risk the flu or whatever virus had befallen poor Izzy and Vanessa. Both women had bad colds, and Axel's sister had already dropped off two get-well baskets of OTC medicine, throat lozenges, boxes of tissues, fuzzy socks and crossword magazines. Daisy had even instructed a ranch hand to drop off three trays of dinner earlier, and the cabin was already equipped with an electric kettle, mugs and tea.

Axel had surprised Sadie and her mom on the porch of the cabin when he told them there was no need to take the porta-crib because he not only had a crib upstairs in the guest room for his visiting baby niece and nephews but also a playpen downstairs in the living room along with various other baby stuff, like a foam play mat and kiddie area in one corner with toys that were probably too young for Danny but that he'd love nonetheless.

"Well," Vanessa had said with a huge smile. "Danny will fit right in over there."

Axel had barely flinched at that, aware of many sets of eyes on him.

Danny was thrilled by the idea of going to Axel's house. And he was practically jumping in his seat when Axel mentioned that Danny could pet his sweet, friendly dog named Dude if he wanted but only if a grown-up was there.

Fifteen minutes later, settled in the cabin, Danny petted Dude over and over and told him a few stories in toddler speak that Axel couldn't make heads or tails out of, but Sadie seemed to understand every word. Then Danny moved over to the play mat in the corner by the window, where there were stuffed toys and cardboard building blocks. Sadie explained that Danny was building a castle for his superhero lion.

"How high are you going to make it?" Axel

asked, sitting cross-legged on the big foam mat. "As tall as you are?"

"Tall you!" Danny said, then doubled over in laughter. Toddler humor.

Danny's laughter was infectious, and both Axel and Sadie were laughing, too. Axel was aware of Sadie watching them from the big brown leather couch that faced the stone fireplace. She was sitting in his favorite spot, the left-hand corner. He suddenly wanted to be sitting right next to her. No, he wanted her on his lap, straddling him, kissing him the way she had in his car, her hands in his hair.

She'd nixed any chance of that—wisely—so keep this G-rated, he reminded himself. *Focus on the kid, not the mother.*

"You're gonna make the castle as tall as I am?" Axel asked Danny. "That *is* tall."

"Zul help?" Danny asked, tilting his head, his hazel-brown eyes wide.

The expression on the adorable little boy's face almost did Axel in with his sweet earnestness. "Of course I'll help."

"Hear-wo," Danny said, smiling. "Right, Mama?"

Oh, God. Now he *was* done in. He wanted to scoop up this kid and give him a big hug. He couldn't look at Danny Winston without remembering the relief he'd felt when he'd followed Dude and spotted the orange sneaker through that thicket of branches. Danny was soothing to be around, even if his occasional high-pitched shrieks could crack double-pane glass.

"Right, Danny," Sadie said with a nod.

Axel kept his gaze on the growing tower of blocks.

Danny yawned and rubbed his eyes, then added another block to the tower.

"It's almost eight o'clock," Sadie said. "His bedtime is seven thirty, but my mom said he took an extralong nap this afternoon. I'd better get him to sleep."

"Time for bed, buddy," Axel said, giving Danny's blond hair a ruffle.

Danny yawned again. "Zul story?" he asked, looking between his mom and Axel.

He looked at Sadie. "He wants me to read him a story?" he asked.

Sadie nodded. "My mom said she packed a few of his favorites. He likes the same ones over and over."

"Sure, I'll read you a story," Axel said.

Danny held out his arms to Axel, and he swallowed. He wasn't expecting that.

"I'll take you up to bed," Sadie said fast, bolting up. "You're going to sleep in Axel's special nursery."

"Zul, Zul!" Danny said, hoisting his arms up toward Axel.

"I don't mind," he whispered to Sadie and then scooped the boy up. "Okay, let's head to bed."

"Zul, too?" Danny asked, looking around. He pointed by the blocks.

His superhero lion lay on the mat beside his castle. Sadie got it and handed it to her son.

"Zul and Zul!" Danny said with glee, flying the lion in his red cape as far as his little arm would allow.

Axel smiled and started up the stairs, Sadie following. He set the boy on the changing table and let his mom get him ready for bed in his spaceship pajamas, then Sadie brought him to the bathroom they'd share for brushing teeth. A few minutes later, Danny came running in with Zul and lifted his arms to Axel. He picked up the boy and sat in the padded rocking chair by the window, and Sadie handed him a picture book.

"Let's see," Axel said. "This book is called *Snowy the Owl*. I love owls, too."

Danny shook his head and waved Zul at Axel. "Story Zul."

Axel was beginning to speak toddler. "Ah, you want a story about Zul the superhero lion?"

Danny nodded and settled in, his head in the crook of Axel's arm, the baby-shampoo scent of him rising up. A pang gripped him in the chest, and he had a flash of the woman he'd loved three years ago sitting in a rocker and reading a story to her baby. Axel had been so attracted to Lizzie, a single mother of an eleven-month-old baby girl, maybe mistaking that for love, and when she'd left him for a bull rider, he'd been out of sorts for months, missing her, missing the baby he'd gotten close to. That was when he'd stopped dating single mothers. It was when he'd stopped dating with an eye toward a future, period. The way he'd felt about Lizzie and her daughter had superseded all the usual reasons he'd never gotten seriously involved with a woman—his upbringing, his cynicism, his lack of faith in people. And then wham, all those walls had built back up even stronger.

Now here he was, sitting on a rocker with a little baby-shampoo-scented kid on his lap, about to make up a story about a superhero lion named after him. This had gotten out of hand.

Whoa, he told himself. *Dial back the intensity. It's a story. You're doing Sadie a favor so she and her son don't get sick. You and Sadie already agreed there would be no more kissing. Don't make this into more than it is.*

Talking-to over, he cleared his throat.

But it already was more because he recognized that what he felt for Sadie Winston was a lot more than lust.

He cleared his throat again and glanced up at Sadie, leaning against the doorway. Waiting.

"Once upon a time, there was a superhero lion named Zul," Axel began.

Danny's eyes were wide on his. So far, so good.

"Zul flew all over the place looking for animals and kids who needed help. One day, Zul saw a little owl who couldn't get back in his nest."

"Oh no!" Danny yelped.

"Don't worry," Axel assured him. "Because Zul was there!"

"Yay, Zul!" Danny said, flying Zul around until a yawn had his arm drooping with his eyes.

"Zul said, 'Hey little owl, hang on to my cape and I'll land you right in your nest.' And Zul did. The little owl was very happy to be home. Zul flew away, his red cape zipping behind, looking to be helpful. The end."

Danny's eyes drooped again, then opened, then drooped hard. A moment later, he managed to get them half-opened, then they closed.

"Good night, little buddy," Axel whispered. There. He'd gotten through this unscathed. He'd told the boy a story and Axel's world hadn't imploded. Mother and child didn't have to affect him if he didn't *let* them.

A few years ago, not long after he'd gotten his heart handed to him by Lizzie, he'd run into Mack, a widowed, grizzled mountain man who'd lived alone for decades in a small cabin he'd built himself. Out of nowhere, the man had said to Axel, finger waving, "I'll tell ya the secret of life, buddy boy. It's ruling your emotions instead of letting them rule you. Be the boss of yourself." Axel had thought that was excellent life advice, not that the mountain man seemed too emotionally healthy and the rangers checked in on him a few times a week. A grown son had been trying to get him to agree to go into assisted living and Mack had put up a fuss, but Axel had heard he'd finally agreed.

He glanced at Sadie, who seemed *very* affected. She was staring at him, and he could swear she might cry.

He carefully stood and walked over to the crib and lowered Danny in, putting Zul under his arm. "Success," he whispered to Sadie. Her eyes were misty. "You okay?"

"You're the first man besides his grandpa to tell Danny a story," she said. "It's very sweet to watch someone tell your baby a story—especially off the cuff. Guess I got a little emotional."

Ah, okay. It was a mother thing and not a *him* thing. Phew. Sadie turned out the light and they left the room, leaving the door ajar.

"Well, I think I'm ready for bed myself," she said, yawning what had to be the fakest yawn he'd ever seen.

She needed some space from him and this—he got it. He did, too.

But he could barely drag his eyes off her, let

alone make his body move farther from hers. If he was honest with himself, he'd admit to wanting to sit with her and talk or watch a movie and eat popcorn. And yes, he wanted to kiss her. More than kiss her.

"If you need anything, just knock," he said, knowing that distance from her was exactly what he needed.

She gave him something of a smile. "Good night," she said. "Thanks for dinner. And for letting us stay here. And for the story."

"My pleasure," he said, holding her gaze. "Pleasant dreams," he added like his grandparents always used to when he was young.

Watching her walk away was so damned hard.

An hour later, Axel lay on his bed, hands folded behind his head, staring at the beamed ceiling. His thoughts were a jumble of everything that had happened that night. The Mexican restaurant. Manuela. The text from Sadie's mom about her and Danny needing to stay at his cabin. Playing with Danny and reading to him. Being so attracted to Sadie that he could barely think of anything without her popping into his mind every five seconds. Her face, her long light blond hair, her pale brown eyes. Her pink lips.

He could not start something with Sadie that wouldn't end with what she wanted; he wouldn't do that to her. She wanted her Mr. Right. He wanted nothing to do with emotional involvement. He was done with love and commitment and caring too much. Yeah, yeah, it had been three years since he had his heart torn out of his chest, but he felt nowhere close to wanting a relationship. Maybe one day the feeling would go away. He had no idea. He knew the idea of getting seriously involved with someone, particularly someone with a child, gave him that airless feeling in his chest.

He wanted the best for Sadie and therefore, he'd keep his hands and lips to himself. Not that she'd invited him to kiss her a second time. She'd made herself crystal clear. She knew what she wanted just as he knew what he didn't want.

He would walk the five miles from his ranch here to sit in her station and have tacos just to see her because she was so busy, he heard Manuela say in his head. *And he never showed up without either flowers or candy. Your mom was a jelly bean addict.*

When Axel and his brothers were young, the three would pool their money on Mother's Day and their mom's birthday and buy Diana Dawson two pounds of jelly beans from the loose candy bins at the general store, trying to avoid the black licorice ones that she hated. They'd each take turns filling the bag and then the lady at the counter would always add a red ribbon and make a bow, and they

were always so proud to hand their mom her gift.
She always shared, too.

*While your parents were dating, I remember
thinking, now that is a man in love...*

Oh hell, he thought, getting up and going over
to his dresser. He sucked in a breath and opened
the sock drawer and pulled out the letter from his
father.

He sat on his bed and opened it. Finally. After
almost nine months.

He pulled out one sheet of plain white paper.
Four addresses were scrawled on it in Bo Dawson's handwriting. Just addresses—all local to Bear
Ridge. None he recognized as remotely familiar.
The first was on Main Street. He grabbed his phone
and did a search for the address—Manuela's Mexican Café.

Huh. The universe had a funny way of getting
someone's attention. He'd never stepped foot in
Manuela's until tonight for the very reason it was
listed on the paper—it had been his father's hang-
out. But he'd gone because Sadie had wanted Mexican, and he'd thought he was being ridiculous for
avoiding a place just because his late father frequented it.

And he'd ended up learning quite a bit about
his parents.

Then had been propelled to finally open the letter from his dad.

He stared at the addresses. So what was this? Bo sending him on some kind of tour of his life? Seemed like it, given what he'd discovered about the first address on the list.

The other three addresses were scattered across the town.

I don't know that I want any more information, he thought.

A memory started to form in his head and he tried to push it away, getting up and dropping the letter on the bed and heading for the window. He looked out over the vast field and trees as it hit him, the night he'd tried so hard not to think about. The universe *had* sent him to Manuela's tonight. The universe *had* gotten him to open up the letter. Maybe he was *supposed* to be thinking of the last time he saw his dad. Even if it crushed him. Talk about stealing the air from his lungs.

One cold December late afternoon, Axel had stopped by the ranch on the way back from training the newbies from the S&R team on easy Clover Mountain. He planned to talk to his dad about rehab. He'd tried a few times before and had gotten nowhere, but Axel had heard from Daisy that she'd been talking to Bo on the phone and he'd been slurring his words, then started snoring. *Nice talking to you, Dad.*

Axel had been researching local rehab facilities and found one that could take Bo that weekend. As he'd pulled up in the drive to the main house, Bo was zigzagging to his truck, which had one caved-in bumper and a lot of new dents. His father was clearly drunk, and Axel had grabbed Bo's keys and refused to hand them over. His father had cursed up a storm, then taken a swing at Axel and fallen flat on his face, passed out cold.

Axel had carried him into the house, no easy feat, got him on the couch, took off his boots and covered him with a blanket. Then Axel had burst into tears.

The crying had helped actually, releasing all that pent-up frustration and anguish and power-lessness. He had no doubt that in the morning, Bo would be up to the same old tricks. Axel had called Noah, who lived second closest to the dilapidated ranch at the time, and told him what happened, and Noah said he'd stop by in the morning and try to talk some sense into Bo. Axel had left and vowed never to return; enough was enough.

That was six days before Bo Dawson died.

Pain clenched at his gut, and he gripped the windowsill, trying to put it all out of his mind, but he couldn't. Noah had reported that their dad had given a repeat performance the next afternoon, down to the punch and passing out, this time in a snowbank in the yard. They'd even gotten their police officer brother involved, Ford coming all the way from Casper in uniform since their father respected any kind of service, whether military or law enforcement or janitorial. Bo hadn't been drunk enough to dare punch a police officer, even his own son, but he'd ordered Ford off his property if he "was going to be a damned killjoy." Ford had let Axel and Noah know the man just wouldn't listen to reason and they couldn't force him into rehab.

The thing that got Axel most? That Bo had obviously known he was dying—the letters he'd left to all six kids made that clear. He'd wanted to go out his way, Axel supposed. And he had.

"Mama? Mama?" a little voice called out.

Axel practically jumped in his dark room. Danny. He went into the hallway, saw no sign of Sadie, so he poked his head into the nursery. Danny was standing up in the crib, holding Zul. The little guy stared at Axel in the dim lighting from the night-light, then popped his arms in the air like he had earlier.

"Can't sleep, huh, buddy?" Axel asked, walking over. "Me neither. Not that I've tried."

Well, he needed a distraction and this was one hell of a distraction.

"How about another story about your superhero lion?" Axel asked, putting Danny on his lap. The boy immediately settled against his chest, his eyes heavy. He'd be out in about half a minute. "Once upon a time there was a lion named Zul. One day,

Zul woke up in the middle of the night, unable to sleep. He wanted someone to tell him a story, but everyone else was sleeping. So he decided to tell *himself* a story. He crawled into his bed, pulled the covers to his chin and told himself about the time he saved a little duckling named George from a fast-moving current in the creek. Before he knew it—"

Axel felt Danny's head press more heavily against the crook of his arm, and he looked down. Bingo: fast asleep. Fourteen seconds. That had to be a record.

"Thanks," he heard Sadie whisper.

He looked up and there she was in the doorway with a sweet smile on her beautiful face. She was barefoot and wore pink sweatpants and a white tank top and looked unbelievably sexy.

"I'll take him to his crib," he said, standing up.

"You're a natural, Axel Dawson. Shame about you not wanting kids of your own." Her eyes widened. "Oh, God, who am I—my mother? I'm really sorry. I had no business saying something like that. People have a right to their feelings without anyone else butting in with their one cent."

"Oh, I wouldn't shortchange yourself," he said and then shut up before he elaborated about how she had this ability to get him talking and thinking and doing things he wouldn't have otherwise.

He'd thought it was the universe's mysterious ways getting him to open the letter.

No. It was the talk he and Sadie had had in the restaurant.

"I'm good with little kids because I had practice," he said, wondering why he was going there. But then he blurted out, "I was seriously involved with a single mother with a baby girl who I was very attached to, and when it was over, I doubled down on my old ways of looking for only casual relationships. So between helping take care of that baby and helping out with my niece and nephews, I've got a ton of experience with the diaper crowd."

"Sorry about the heartache. I know how that goes. And thanks to my great-gram, I know you know I do."

He smiled. "They're a great family. You're lucky."

"Well, I've only met two of your five siblings, but I'd say you're darn lucky yourself."

"That is true," he agreed. "I lucked out in that department, at least."

He moved closer to her—to leave the room so that Danny could sleep in peace, but she was right there, in the doorway, and suddenly they were kissing again. She'd made the first move and he'd made the second and now they were in the hallway against the wall about to knock over the watercolor of rushing rapids. Now he knew where that part of the Zul story had come from.

"Why can't I keep my hands off you?" she whispered against his lips, pressed up tantalizingly against him.

"Feel free not to," he said, then regretted it. Even if he was attracted to her on a bunch of levels—okay, all—he wasn't getting emotionally attached.

She seemed to sense his withdrawal despite his not moving a muscle. "Maybe we should save the making out for when my family is around," she said, and he heard the element of disappointment in her voice. He was getting to know her a little too well. "You know, to make the engagement seem real. We were supposed to talk about that and never did. But now I'm zonked," she said, fake-yawning again and backing toward her room. "So, see you in the morning."

She hurried down the hall, and her door closed a second later.

He could knock and they could talk, really talk. But his feet were suddenly weighted to the floor, and Sadie had fled for a reason. He should let her be.

Wasn't getting emotionally attached. Even he knew when he was full of it.

Chapter Eight

When Sadie woke up the next morning and eyed the time on her phone, she was surprised it was past seven. Danny's middle-of-the-night story must have had him sleep in. She went into the nursery but the crib was empty, which meant only one thing—

"We're making pancakes," called Axel's voice. "Morning, sleepyhead."

Toddler laughter. "Mama sleephead. Hahaha-hahaha."

She smiled, that sound her favorite of every sound in the world.

"I've got him, so feel free to take your time,"

Axel called up. "I'm not expected at work until nine for a wilderness tour."

"'K, thanks," she called out.

"Mama, sleephead!" Danny shouted with glee.

"Well, she's awake now!" Axel said and it was apparently very funny because Danny started laughing again.

"Should we put blueberries in our pancakes?" Axel asked. "Or have them on the side? So many questions!"

"In, in!" Danny said.

Sadie stood at the base of the stairs, smiling and wanting to cry at the same time. This was what life would be like if Danny had a daddy—the right daddy. One who'd get up early with him. Make him a good breakfast. Make him laugh.

This is what I want for my son, she knew more than she knew anything else. And the man being the "right daddy" this morning wasn't available for the permanent position. He was a temp. This week only.

As Sadie passed the watercolor of the rushing rapids on her way to the guest room, she remembered her shoulder tipping it askew, Axel's tall, strong, warm body against hers on the wall, his hands on her shoulders, her neck as he kissed her. She'd practically flung herself at him—not even practically. She had. Seeing him in the rocker, taking care of Danny in the middle of the night, telling him that story. She'd been overcome, and added to how attracted she was to him, she'd let impulse win.

You've got to stop that, she told herself as she went into the bathroom with the toiletry bag her mother had packed for her and took a shower, grateful for the excellent water pressure on her tense muscles. Axel had everything in here a guest could need, including a hair dryer. Once in her room, she got dressed in a T-shirt and shorts, then texted her mom to see how Gram and Great-Gram were doing. Her mother ruled against visiting so she wouldn't get Danny or Axel sick and thought they'd be much better by tomorrow.

Downstairs, she found Danny in a high chair near the table. Axel had made smiley face blueberry pancakes. The mouth was strawberry slices.

"Hi, sleephead!" Danny said and laughed again.

"Hi, precious," Sadie responded, kissing Danny on the head. "Mmm, your breakfast looks delicious."

"And here is yours, milady," Axel said, putting a plate on the table. Three pancakes. A side of blueberries and strawberries. Syrup, butter, orange juice and cream and sugar were in the center, and then he set down a steaming mug of coffee.

Everyone needed an Axel. The man really was a superhero.

"Noah texted," he said. "Turns out Daisy needs

help with something at her house, so I'll see you two later." He gave Danny's hair a ruffle.

"Bye, Zul!" Danny said, waving his pancake-laden fork in the air.

Axel smiled. "See you later, buddy." He turned toward Sadie. "I don't know what time I'll be back, but make yourself at home, come and go as you please."

Her heart pinged. "Thanks for everything, Axel."

He nodded and then was gone.

"I like Zul," Danny said, picking up his sippy cup.

"Me, too," she said. "Me, too."

Turned out a bird had somehow gotten into Daisy's house over an hour ago and she needed help shooing it out. Her husband, Harrison, was on a business trip for the next few days, and though Noah and Sara lived just down the path in the foreman's cabin, they were already out dealing with feed deliveries, so Axel was now bird shooer.

"Where's Tony?" Axel asked, glancing around for his three-month-old nephew.

"He's napping upstairs in his crib. Good timing, too, because I can just imagine the bird pooping on his head. It's been that kind of day and it's not even eight a.m."

Whoosh!

There the little bird went, flying not too far

overhead. It was brown, gray and white and flying around Daisy's living room. She'd opened the sliding glass doors and all the windows but birdie seemed to prefer flying against the walls instead of into freedom.

"I summon all the powers of Zul to mind-trick this bird out the side door!" Axel said in his best Darth Vader voice.

"Um, who?" Daisy asked, staring at him as if he'd grown another head.

"Zul. Danny's superhero lion," he said.

Daisy's mouth dropped open. "Oh, my God. You're falling for Sadie and you adore that kid!"

"What? I'm trying to get the bird out of your house."

Daisy raised an eyebrow. "Yes, by calling on the imaginary powers of a two-year-old's stuffed lovey. Oh, Axel. You're a goner."

He frowned at his sister, who he'd never told about Lizzie, and followed the bird with his gaze. Now it was flying along the ceiling. "We're talking about *me*, remember? Or have you forgotten I'm the guy who actually caused his blind date to go running out of your dinner party."

He felt bad about that one. A few months ago, Daisy had slyly set him up with the woman who used to lead wilderness tours for the ranch, and he'd been wound so tight in those days that he'd gotten into an argument with Daisy's husband—

who'd been the family's enemy back then—and the date had fled. She'd also quit not long after, taking a job with his old S&R team. That had worked out well, since he'd taken over as wilderness tour leader and safety director for the ranch.

Whoosh! Whoosh-whoosh!

Ah—birdie flew out the sliding glass door.

"Phew," Daisy said, hurrying to close the windows and the doors. She turned toward him. "Axel Dawson, you can say whatever you want. Actions speak louder."

She had him there. "Maybe I shouldn't tell you that Sadie and Danny are staying with me for a couple of days. Her grandmother and great-grandmother have bad colds, so Sadie's mom is taking care of them at their cabin and sent her daughters to their fiancés."

Daisy grinned. "Oh, what a tangled web—wonderfully tangled!"

"I don't know how wonderful it is, Daize. First off, it *is* deception. Second, yeah, I do have feelings for Sadie, and, of course, I feel close to her son—Dude and I found him when he was missing. But I'm not looking for a relationship. I don't *want* a relationship."

"Why do you think you can control that?" she asked, shaking her head.

Be the boss of yourself, he heard the mountain

man say. *Rule your emotions instead of letting them rule you.*

Now that he thought about it, though, Axel realized he was hardly the boss of his emotions. "I'm not pronouncing it out of nowhere—it's just how I *feel*, Daisy."

"Exactly. Because the heart is mightier than the head. Just accept it."

Okay, now he was confused. "What I'll accept is a cup of coffee," he said. "The chocolaty-hazelnut kind you gave me the other day, if you still have some."

She narrowed her blue eyes on him. "Changing the subject, I see. And yes, I always have chocolate-hazelnut."

He followed her to the big country kitchen, and Axel leaned against the counter. "I opened my letter from Dad."

Daisy gasped and turned to him. "Um, Axel, you could have led with that. What did it say?"

"It actually didn't say anything. Just a piece of paper with four Bear Ridge addresses. That's it. No explanations, no annotations."

She added the coffee grounds into the filter and hit Brew. "Really? Recognize any of them?"

"Turns out, completely by coincidence, I went to one last night." He explained about the grandmother and great-grandmother ambushing him into taking his fiancée out to dinner. "I walked in the door of Manuela's Mexican Café, and the owner took one look at me and knew I had to be Bo Dawson's son. She told me that's where he met my mom—when she was a waitress there."

"Wow," Daisy said. She poured his coffee, added cream and two teaspoons of sugar and handed the mug to him.

"Thanks," he said, lifting the mug. He took a long sip. "Apparently, Dad was so in love with her that when her car broke down, he gave her his truck so she could get to school and work, and he'd walk five miles from the ranch to see her. Then back. He brought her candy and flowers."

"Bo had a good side, Axel. We know that. My mom was madly in love with him despite his flaws."

Daisy and Noah's mother had come along not long after Axel's had had enough of Bo's hard-living ways—drinking, gambling, staying out late, flirting and no doubt cheating. Axel and his brothers had adored their stepmother, Leah, who was kind and compassionate and treated them like they were special. He'd never forget that. He'd been devastated when she'd died. Axel had been thirteen, Daisy eleven, Noah nine. Axel's mother hadn't been comfortable letting him and his brothers visit their father longer than a day with just Bo supervising. As teenagers, they'd barely seen him at all except for occasions, and he never failed to let them down in big and small ways that had stung.

Now he had a list of four addresses.

"So you think the other addresses will tell a story, too?" she asked.

"I have a feeling, yes. Not sure I want to hear it, though."

"You don't, but you do. That's always the way it is with complicated stuff, Axel."

Didn't he know it.

For the next couple of hours, Sadie and Danny explored the grounds around Axel's gorgeous log cabin. They'd found a hammock in the side yard, and she and Danny had stretched out for a while, soaking up the beautiful September sunshine before Danny got bored and wanted to run around, flying Zul. Then they'd met up with family for an early lunch at the cafeteria, Danny gobbling up the chili and corn bread. As always, there were multiple kid zones in the lodge, for the under-five, under-twelve and the teen set, and so she'd watched Danny have a blast in the toddler playground. The kid rooms were supervised, which was nice because there was also a refreshment table offering coffee, and Sadie needed some.

Ping.

A text from her sister: I hear you're staying at Axel's for a couple of days till Gram and Great-

Gram are better. How about if Marshall and I bring dinner over tonight? We can pick up from the caf or bring in Thai or Italian—whatever you guys want. I've been craving pasta like crazy lately.

Sadie swallowed. She loved the idea of texting back, Sure, and get pasta carbonara for me, penne in butter and cheese for Danny and baked ziti for Axel. Oh, and garlic bread.

She knew Axel loved baked ziti and garlic bread because they'd talked about their favorites last night. *I could eat five servings of even meh baked ziti myself*, he'd said.

She sucked in a breath and texted: My sister has invited herself and her fiancé over to your house for dinner tonight, but they're bringing the food. Italian? Baked ziti for you and tiramisu for dessert?

She hit Send and looked to see what Danny was doing. He was sitting at a little table with a staff member, coloring a picture. She eyed her phone. Nothing.

A full minute later, still nothing.

He's busy, for God's sake. He's on a wilderness tour and is responsible for the safety of several of your relatives. Except the trek was at nine and it was now past two.

She imagined him reading her text and thinking: *She's going too far. She and Danny were foisted on me and now she's arranging dinner get-*

*togethers at my house with her family? It's getting
to be much too much.*

Her stomach hurt.

Ping.

Sounds good. Don't forget the garlic bread.—A

He'd added the smiley face emoji in the cowboy hat again.

Her heart did five backflips.

She texted Evie to let her know they were in and
their orders. As she finally pocketed her phone, her
cousin Daphne, who'd been on the hiking trip on
Badger Mountain that fateful day Danny had gone
missing, came up to the table and poured herself
a coffee. She'd been pregnant then and now had a
baby girl named Bea.

"Daph, has my mom or Tabby ever talked to
you about what happened between them that day
on the mountain?"

Daphne pushed her long red hair behind her
shoulders, then added cream to the cup. "They're
still in a fight? Jeez. I remember them arguing
while the search crew was looking for Danny but
I didn't hear what they were saying since I was so
focused on the search. I sure hope they make up
this week. I mean, how can they not?"

"That's my hope, too. I'm about to go see my

mom—she's taking care of Gram and Great-Gram, who have colds."

"Hey, my sister and I are about to take her kids over to the petting zoo. I'm happy to take Danny along if you want a break."

Sadie smiled. "I'll bet he'd love to go with you guys. Text me when you're ready to leave the zoo and I'll come pick him up." She walked over to where Danny was admiring his drawing of Zul.

"Look, Mommy!"

She kneeled and smiled at the drawing. "It's Zul, saving the day. I love it. Hey, I'm going to see your grandma right now. Want me to give it to her as a present from you?"

Danny beamed. "Yes!"

"And while I do that, do you want to go to the petting zoo and see the animals with cousins Daphne and Lauren and their kids?"

"Yay, petting zoo!" Danny scrambled off the chair and ran straight to Daphne, where the group was waiting.

"Have fun!" Sadie called, blowing a kiss. She waved at Daphne and watched the group leave, finished her coffee and then headed out for her cabin. She hoped to run into her "fiancé" while she was walking but she didn't see him anywhere. She saw his brother Noah and his wife, Sara, the forewoman, and gave them a wave, but no Axel. What she would give to drink in the sight of him…

She made her way the quarter mile down the path to her cabin. The guest quarters managed to be secluded and not at the same time. Each cabin was spaced far enough apart that you couldn't see the others, trees giving privacy. Sadie loved the woodsy setting and breathed in the fresh scent of pine and flowers and earth.

As she rounded the cabin to the front, she saw her aunt Tabby stomping angrily away, her shoulder-length auburn hair bouncing behind her. Uh-oh.

"Tabby?" Sadie called out. "You okay?"

Her aunt turned and marched over, tears and anger in her eyes. "No, I most certainly am not! Vanessa and Izzy are my mom and grandmother, too, not that your mother seems to remember that!" She stalked off before Sadie could say another word, then ran back and kissed Sadie on the cheek. "I don't mean to take out my frustration on you, Sades. Love you! Toodles!" Then she stalked away again, and Sadie could see her swiping under her eyes.

Oh, dear.

Sadie shook her head as she walked up the cabin steps and knocked since her mother had texted five times she should do so instead of coming to "cold central."

"Coming!" she heard her mother call.

Viv opened the door and frowned. "Honey, this

is sick bay. You can't be here! You'll get sick, then Danny will, then Axel will!"

She held up the drawing. "I'm dropping this off. Danny drew it and wanted you to have it."

Her mother smiled. "Love that boy. And so talented. I'll put it on the minifridge for now. Shoo now, before the germs get you."

"You have those germs all over you, Mom," Sadie pointed out. "And you don't seem to have caught their colds."

"I just don't want a cold getting in the way of you spending this quality time with Axel or you and Evie making plans for the weddings. Nothing is worse than feeling rotten with a cold, honey."

"Ain't that the truth," Vanessa called out in a congested voice. Sadie heard her blow her nose— loudly.

"Aw, poor Gram and Great-Gram." She lowered her voice. "Look, Mom, I truly appreciate that you care about me. But, I ran into Tabby leaving and *I'm* not leaving this porch until you tell me what is going on between you two. What happened, Mom? You have to tell me because it's my fault."

Viv frowned and then looked sad. "How is it your fault?"

"You know why. You and Tabby stopped talking the day Danny went missing."

"That's not your fault. It's Tabby's—" She clamped her mouth shut.

"Aha!" Sadie said. "So you blame her for Danny going missing?"

"I hear Izzy calling for me," Viv lied. "You can't keep an ill ninety-nine-year-old waiting when she wants her chicken soup."

"Mom, c'mon. This is our family reunion. Were you trying to shut Tabby out of helping nurse her own mother and grandmother? She's their daughter, too."

"So *everyone* should get sick?" Viv asked. "Tabby's the one who wanted to stay with our cousins instead of bunking with us like she always does at the reunions. So tough noogies."

"Mom, seriously."

"I'm being serious as a you-know-what." Viv stepped aside. "Toodles, hon. Say hi to Axel and kiss my darling grandbaby for your ole ma, will you?"

The door closed.

Could her mother *be* more frustrating? How could two grown women who used phrases like "Toodles" be so stubborn?

Some family reunion. Her mother and aunt weren't speaking. Her grandmother and great-grandmother were sick with colds, and Sadie couldn't visit with them if she wanted to keep the peace with her mom. And Sadie's whole world had turned upside down with one little white lie.

At least Sadie knew she had pasta carbonara in her future. And garlic bread. And Axel.

Chapter Nine

As was the case these days, Axel both liked and didn't like that Sadie was sitting on the living room carpet with Danny next to the tower of blocks when he got home. Like they lived there. Like they were his family. His wife, his child.

He got that discomfort in his chest, as though air was squeezing out. But at the same time, good goose bumps traveled up his spine at the sight of beautiful Sadie and her sweet toddler, whom he had to admit he adored. When he'd worked at Badger Mountain, he was used to coming home to an empty house with Dude, his partner on his missions, and then it would be just the two of them unless he went out with some of his colleagues on the search and rescue team. He'd tended to save that for only events—birthdays and welcomes and retirements. So it was always just him and Dude in his cabin, first the small one and now here at the ranch.

Then again, these past weeks, being right on the property, he found himself spending a lot of time with his brother and sister and their families—and liking it. For the longest time, the thought of the Dawson Family Guest Ranch had reminded him of his father, of bad times. But now, the place made him think of his baby niece and nephews, of dinners with his siblings and their spouses, commiserating on tough days when there were guest injuries or issues, laughing at Daisy's funny stories, feeling grateful when Noah would talk about those months he and a team had spent rebuilding the family ranch into something new but that still paid homage to their grandparents.

Axel had been changing without even realizing it, he now knew.

"Zul!" Danny said as Axel came inside, leaping up and careening straight for him. The little boy wrapped his arms around Danny's legs, and Axel scooped him up, hoisting him high.

"Building Zul's tower, I see," Axel said. "Looks

great." He put Danny on the ground and the boy ran to his blocks, toddler-telling him all about it.

Sadie smiled up at him. "Evie and Marshall will be here at seven with Italian from Figorella's. I love that place."

"Not in Bear Ridge, right? I haven't heard of it."

"Prairie City. My parents go every Friday night."

The small talk made him aware of how strange this was. This woman and child in his house, staying with him till at least tomorrow. Her family coming over as their guests.

It's just till tomorrow. They'll head for the cabin. At the end of the week, they'll return to Prairie City. This will all be over.

And you'll be on your own again.

The idea of them leaving didn't sit right either, though.

For the next hour there was tower building and then Sadie gave Danny his bath, and then it was Zul story time, so once again, he settled Danny on his lap, the baby-shampoo scent of him reminding him of another time, another child, and again, the air seeped.

Another single mother in the doorway, watching, seemingly happy.

Seemingly. Interesting. Was he expecting Sadie to pull a fast one on him? They weren't even in a real relationship. He was losing his mind, clearly.

Maybe it had just been a long day.

With Danny tuckered out and in his crib, fast asleep within minutes, they tiptoed out of the nursery and went downstairs. Her sister and her real fiancé would be here any minute. Danny had eaten earlier and Sadie had mentioned she'd put his penne in the fridge for tomorrow's lunch.

Axel was starving. And looking forward to the baked ziti and garlic bread and tiramisu.

"You two are such a great couple," Evie whispered after dinner as Axel got up from the table to collect the empty tiramisu dishes. Marshall hopped to it as well, and the men brought the dishes and silverware into the kitchen.

"He's a good guy," Sadie whispered in turn, not surprised she and Axel had come across as a real couple during dinner.

They talked so easily, were truly interested in what the other had to say, and Axel had cute stories to tell about putting Danny to bed and building towers. He really did seem like Sadie's fiancé and Danny's dad-to-be. To the point that at times during dinner, Sadie had almost forgotten he *wasn't*. And he was warm and friendly to her sister and Marshall, sharing memories about growing up on a dude ranch and about his work as a search and rescue specialist. Evie was in love with Dude and couldn't stop petting him. The Lab had spent the meal under her feet for that reason.

"It's so obvious how much you two care about each other," Evie added, then took a sip of her coffee. "The way he looks at you—warms my heart. With such love and respect."

Well, he did seem to respect her but he certainly didn't love her.

Evie's diamond ring twinkled on her finger as she covered Sadie's hand with her own. "I'm so happy for you and Danny, Sadie. You truly found a real hero."

Okay, a crummy weight lodged in Sadie's heart. She wanted this to be real. She wanted Axel to be her and Danny's hero, and for her and Danny to be *his* heroes. She needed a little rescuing in some ways and so did Axel. And she was up for the job.

If only, if only, if only.

As the guys came back, Sadie thanked them for being on table-clearing duty, and they went into the living room and plopped down on the comfortable sofa with their coffees.

"So I brought this fun game," Evie said, getting up and walking over to the foyer where she brought in a paper bag. She sat and pulled out a bright red box. The Love Game: So You Think You Know Your Significant Other?

Uh-oh. Party games could be fun but this one was going to be a disaster. *Please don't let there be embarrassing questions about sex*, she thought, bracing herself for the worst and most mortifying.

"Okay," Evie said, taking the lid off the box and pulling out stacks of cards. "We each get three cards with a letter on it—A, B and C." She handed those out. "These are our answer cards for the multiple-choice questions. We keep those hidden from one another. Then, we take turns picking a face-down question card from the stack. Each card has a multiple-choice question for you to answer about your partner. After you read the question aloud, your partner chooses from the three possible answer cards—A, B or C—and places his answer card facedown in front of him. Then *you* answer. If you two are in sync, you get ten points. If not, you lose ten points. The losing couple treats the winning couple to dinner next time!"

Sadie glanced at Axel. He didn't look miserable or like he wanted to crush the cards in his hand into dust. That was good.

"Who wants to go first?" Evie asked.

Sadie swallowed. *Not me.* Axel didn't shoot his hand in the air either.

No one seemed eager, not even Marshall, who presumably knew his fiancée well after three years.

"Guess I'll go first!" Evie said, taking a sip of her coffee, then picking up the top card from the face-down stack. "'Your partner forgot your birthday. Will your partner, A, Say, oh, sorry, happy birthday, by the way. B, Rush out and buy you a card and gift. C, As if my partner would forget my birthday—puhleeeze!' Okay, so Marshall, now you choose either an A, B or C card as your answer and put that card facedown. Then I'll answer."

Marshall eyed his cards and swished his mouth around. "Hmm," he said. "Okay, got it." He put a card face down on his knee.

"The only possible answer is C," Evie said. "As if I'd let you forget! Am I right, Marsh?"

Marshall grinned and triumphantly held up the C card.

"Well done," Axel said to him.

Evie beamed. "Okay, we'll go clockwise, so it's your turn, Sadie."

Sadie glanced at Axel, then picked up a card. "'Your partner comes home with an adorable puppy in a cardboard box. You're a cat person. You, A, Instruct your partner to find another home for it ASAP. B, Bring it to the animal shelter. C, Name your new puppy and welcome him to the family.'" All eyes turned to Axel. He quickly chose his answer card and put it on his knee. "I'm going with C," Sadie said.

Axel didn't know her well enough to know what a sappy soft heart she was, right? As if she could not immediately fall in love with a little or even big puppy with its sweet puppy eyes. Axel was probably the same. Or maybe he knew her better than she thought.

Her faux fiancé smiled and held up the C card. "Dude turned Sadie into a dog person."

"I happen to love both dogs *and* cats," Sadie said, a little too happy that she and Axel had earned their ten points.

Marshall picked a card and turned to his fiancée. "'I'll be away on a transcontinental business trip for two months. We'll keep the love alive by, A, Cheating to remind us that we prefer each other by the time I return. B, Lots of video calls, phone convos, texts with heart emojis and as many visits as we can. C, As if I'd ever leave you behind.'"

Evie chose her answer card, keeping the letter hidden against her chest.

"Is that your final answer?" Marshall asked.

"It's my final answer," Evie said, patting Dude, who'd curled up beside her.

"First of all," Marshall began, "I would never, ever, ever cheat on Evie. I'm lucky enough to have her. Second, if a business trip does call me away for two months, which will feel like forever, I would FaceTime every night, call, text and hope Evie would visit as often as she could. Not being able to leave each other's side doesn't sound so healthy."

Evie grinned and held up her B card.

"Yes!" Marshall said, high-fiving his fiancée.

"Your turn, Axel," Evie said.

He took a long sip of his coffee, then picked up a card. Was it her imagination or did he flinch slightly as he read it to himself?

Uh-oh. That meant the question was either embarrassing or too personal.

Axel cleared his throat. "'Your partner wants five kids. You're not sure you want kids at all. You, A, Assure your partner that compromise is the name of the game. B, Tell your partner it's over. C, Get them upstairs to the bedroom pronto." Axel didn't look at Sadie. He kept his gaze somewhere between his lap and his coffee mug.

"Oooh, hard one," Evie commented. "I mean, if one partner doesn't want kids and the other wants five... Even compromising on two could be impossible. One wants a big family and the other doesn't want kids at all."

"That's a toughie," Marshall agreed. "Evie and I both want at least three, so phew," he added.

Sadie bit her lip. She wanted the answer to be A. She needed the answer to be A. But only because Axel didn't want *any* kids. Compromise *was* the name of the game—most of the time. But some things were deal breakers for good reason in relationships. Not wanting kids could be one of those.

Then again, Axel didn't want to get *married*.

"I'm not sure," Sadie said, picking up her coffee cup and taking a long sip.

"Well, pick your answer based on what you think Axel's answer is," Evie suggested. "That should make it easier."

Yeah, it did. But he wouldn't choose B—*tell your partner it's over*. Not during a "love" game with her sister and her fiancé when she and Axel were supposed to be a madly-in-love engaged couple themselves.

She looked up at Axel—and felt instantly better. He was sitting there, all handsome and agreeable and kind, his piercing blue eyes grazing over her before he plucked a chocolate chip cookie off the plate on the table. She *did* know him, she realized. He wasn't going to pick A, the one about compromising. He'd pick C, the lighthearted answer about making whoopee to make babies. It was the "right" answer for the game, for the situation, for the present company. Even if he didn't mean it. Just like he didn't mean that they were engaged. It was all pretend.

Pretend, pretend, pretend.

"My answer is C," Sadie said, suddenly not having much fun.

"Is that your final answer?" Marshall asked with a grin.

"Yes," Sadie said, trying to inject some levity into her voice.

"Okay, Axel, is my sister right?" Evie asked.

"Of course she is," he said, turning the card over and showing everyone the C.

Sadie wanted to cry. Because it meant she'd been right about knowing him, understanding him. And because he was lying through his very nice teeth.

And she *did* want five kids. Okay, three, like her sister and brother-in-law-to-be. Two for sure. But Axel had made it crystal clear he wanted *no* kids. No wife. No forever.

The game moved on, the questions a little easier on Sadie's heart and mind when it wasn't her turn. They played for another forty minutes or so, but then Evie started yawning and Danny let out a "Mama?" from the nursery, and they were hugging Evie and Marshall goodbye.

"Next time, our place to finish the game!" Evie said, waving as she and Marshall headed down the porch steps.

Suddenly it was just the two of them. Now Sadie wished her sister and Marshall were here as buffers. Because she had no right to be upset. The man was not her fiancé!

Danny had quieted for a minute there, and either he'd fallen back to sleep or was waiting for her to come. "Mama?" he called again. "Zul?"

Sadie's heart clenched. He was also calling for Axel. Her son adored the man. It went beyond naming a superhero lion after the man who saved him on the mountain.

Oh, boy. What had she done? After this week, when Axel disappeared from Danny's life, how did she think the little boy was going to react to that? Why had she put her own son in a position to be hurt by his hero?

She closed her eyes for a second and then dashed upstairs, willing herself not to cry. Putting her own heart in jeopardy was one thing— Danny's was off-limits to that.

"Sadie? You okay?" Axel asked from behind her.

She didn't respond.

"Sadie," he said again, putting a hand on her shoulder at the landing.

She whirled around. "Many nights my son calls for me when he wakes up and can't soothe himself back to sleep. But tonight he also called for *you*."

He froze for a second. "Because he knows he's in my house. That's all. He knows I'm here."

"He's two years old. All he knows is that 'Zul' is in his life, intensely suddenly. He doesn't understand context. And when we leave, not just your house, Axel, but the ranch and your life, he's going to be very confused." Tears stung her eyes.

"Zul?" Danny called.

Now tears slipped down her cheeks. "Let's go in. We can talk after."

He gently reached up a hand as if to wipe away the tears, but she turned away and headed into the nursery.

"Zul," Danny said, shooting his arms up toward Axel. Sadie could tell that Danny was tired and probably had had a strange dream that had woken him up. A little soothing and he'd be asleep in no time.

Axel glanced at her—for permission, she realized—and she let out a breath and nodded, her heart splintering.

As Axel picked up Danny and cuddled him close, rubbing his back, Danny said, "Dada," and then his eyes closed.

Sadie gasped under her breath.

Dada.

Axel had gone stock-still.

Danny had fallen asleep, and Axel walked him around the nursery a couple of times, then paced in front of the crib before gently lowering him. Danny stirred and pulled Zul under his arm, then his little chest was rising up and down, up and down.

Sadie hurried out of the nursery and Axel followed, keeping the door slightly ajar. She rushed down the stairs and stood in the middle of the hall, her arms crossed over her chest. Axel came down slowly, staring at her, his hands shoved in the pockets of his jeans.

"We'll leave in the morning," she said. "Enough is enough. I'll explain the misunderstanding about the engagement to my family and they'll have to get over it. Danny comes first here. He called you Dada. *Dada*," she repeated. "That's a big problem, as you know. A big confusing problem for Danny. And it's my job to protect him from things like that." She shook her head, tears stinging.

He didn't say anything. Just nodded—miserably.

"Well," she said, lifting her chin. "I'll go clean up. I need to do something with all this…angst, so don't try to be nice and stop me."

"Okay," he said. "Can I at least help?"

She burst into tears.

Axel stepped forward and pulled her into his arms and though part of her knew she should run into the kitchen and start scrubbing, she let herself have this. She sagged against him, wrapping her arms around him. The hug, warm, tight, was so comforting. "Whatever you need, Sadie. What Danny needs. That's all I've ever cared about."

That was only partially true. They *needed* to complete their very small family—a loving, committed life partner for Sadie, a dad for Danny. Axel had taken himself out of the running for that.

"No matter what, Sadie, everything is going to be okay. Know why?"

She looked up at him. "Why?"

"Because you're a great mom."

She swiped under her eyes and felt herself calming. "I'm trying to be. But I messed up here. I should never have let this lie go on. And tonight? Full-out lying in my sister's face?" She shook her head. "Evie is my best friend. What am I doing?"

"You got caught in a crazy moment and you went with each subsequent moment and the moments snowballed. You're doing this for Evie. Remember that. You would have come clean, but then she said all that stuff about not wanting to get engaged until you found your Mr. Right."

"I know, but..." But what? She was going to march over to the cabin in the morning and announce she let them all believe a lie? That she'd gone to a bridal boutique and played a game meant for couples when she was really as single-Sadie as ever?

Yes, dammit. Because her son was calling her fake fiancé *Dada*. And that was the deal breaker.

Your toddler calls your faux fiancé Dada. Do you, A, Let your precious son believe that when nothing could be further from the truth. B, Tell everyone you're a big fat liar. C, There is no good answer.

She was going with B. She had to tell the truth.

Evie's wedding was at the end of the week. The truth would make her sister feel like dog doo and she'd be furious at Sadie for perpetuating the lie, for not telling at least *her* the truth when they were so close. Her mother would cry. Vanessa would have to call everyone she knew and would never get off the phone for the rest of the family reunion. Izzy, beloved Great-Gram, would be confused. Her mom and Aunt Tabby would go back to not even trying to be civil around each other for the sake of the engaged Winston sisters.

And Danny would ask where Zul was. When he'd see him.

What a mess. She could clean up the one in the kitchen by putting the dishes in the dishwasher and tossing the take-out containers in the trash.

"How can I not tell everyone the truth?" she asked him.

"This is one time I wish I was a superhero. That I could turn back time to the second Izzy thought we were the engaged ones, and neither of us said otherwise. But—"

"But you can't and neither can I."

"Actually, I was going to say, but then I—" He stopped again and stared at the floor, then at the window in the hall, then at Dude, who was staring at them.

"Then you what?" she asked, holding still. Then he *what*?

"Then I wouldn't have gotten to know you, Sadie. And I like what I know. I wouldn't have gone to Manuela's Mexican Café. I wouldn't have opened the letter from my dad after almost nine months of being scared to death of it."

She almost gasped. She hadn't expected him to say anything like that.

"You opened the letter?" she repeated. "Did it work the same magic that Daisy's and Noah's did for them?"

"I don't know yet. It's a list of four addresses. Nothing else. Just addresses. Manuela's was one of them."

"He's sending you on an explanation of his life," she said slowly. "Oh, Axel. I think that's what you need to make peace with all that happened between you two."

"I was thinking that maybe I'd check out another of the addresses tomorrow. But—"

She waited.

"I accidentally went to one of the addresses with you the other night and it helped, having you there to talk to about everything. Given that I don't know what the next place will be or what it will call up in me, I'd appreciate having you there. Again. I mean, if you want."

"Of course I want."

He pulled her into his arms again and hugged her. "Thank you," he whispered. He turned to Dude. "Time for a long walk, partner." He looked at Sadie again. "You okay about being here alone for about half an hour?"

She nodded. "I could use the alone time right now. For about that long."

"Me, too," he said.

Then he and Dude were out the front door, taking her heart with them.

Chapter Ten

Axel woke up with the roosters the next morning, not that the ranch had roosters because they would wake up the guests at 4:30 a.m. He wanted to be out before Sadie and Danny left, and he didn't want Sadie to feel that she had to say goodbye, which would be weird and confusing for Danny. He'd make a point of running into them on the ranch later and he'd give Danny closure. He wasn't sure what, but he'd think of something. Something to assure him that even though the tyke wouldn't be seeing Axel much, Axel would always be thinking of him.

Damn. That part was true. He would always be thinking of Danny. The little kid had gotten inside him. And so had his mother.

Last night had almost done him in. The after-dinner game. The question about kids—and he'd answered as he'd known Sadie would have liked, but it had cost him. That lie hadn't been a momentary blip that he could forget about. It served to remind him that Sadie did want a bigger family than she had right now, one that included a husband and siblings for Danny.

And then Danny had called for him. And squeezed the air from Axel's lungs even harder by calling him *Dada*.

Dada. Axel.

He'd returned from a walk with Dude, who could roam loose around the property near his cabin. This was all Dawson land, and guests never ventured this far out even when lost. The walk hadn't done him any good. His shoulders were just as bunched up as when he'd left. He'd been hoping and not hoping—his life story—that Sadie would still be in the kitchen or maybe reading or watching TV in the living room so that they'd be forced to deal with each other, to talk. But the cabin had been quiet and Sadie's door was closed. He'd peeked in on Danny and found Sadie asleep in the yellow glider on the moon-and-stars rug in the nursery, a throw half covering her.

He'd stood there staring at her for a good minute, his heart moving in his chest, the air seeping
in and out of his lungs, whatever *that* meant, and
he knew he wouldn't be walking away from Sadie
Winston so easily. He had…feelings for her. And
he adored her son. He'd have to deal with that.

But she was going to tell her family the truth
today. Unless he could save her from the fallout by
magically proposing to her for real. But he couldn't
do that. He wasn't up for a real relationship with
real expectations and real emotions. At least in
this faux engagement he could pretend—and pretending was easy.

He stopped at the ranch cafeteria for breakfast
before the daily staff meeting at seven and poked
his head in. Yes. The place had just opened and not
a Winston was here yet. If any had been here and
saw him sitting alone, they'd insist he join them
and that would create more weirdness later, once
word spread that they weren't engaged.

How was she going to tell her family the truth?
So damn awkward. And he knew she'd be morti-
fied for a good long time. Dang it.

He went up to the counter, where a long, polished wood bar separated the dining area from
the kitchen. He waved at Cowboy Joe and the two
cooks working on bacon and sausage. Fran, in her
hunter green polo, sat in her tall-backed chair at
the counter, ready to tap his order into her com-

puter tablet. She was seventy and a whiz at her job, keeping the line moving. Axel had a smile for Fran, despite not feeling it. He went with the famed blueberry pancakes and a side of bacon. Coffee and orange juice were on a self-serve station to the side, and he planned to refill at least three times.

He took his order ticket and got himself coffee and juice, then sat at a table by a window, heart weighed down with at least five bricks. Was Sadie texting her mom right now? *I have something to tell you.*

He hated the idea of her dealing with all this on her own. The telling, the confused stares, the *Oh, Sadie, how could you?*

He sure did seem to care about her.

Axel pulled out his phone and texted her: You could always tell them that we decided to call off the engagement, that we want to give the relationship more time. You don't have to say we never were a couple, let alone never engaged.

He set aside his phone, sipped his coffee and waited for a ping. He had no doubt she was awake, probably getting Danny ready for the day in his favorite dinosaur T-shirt and orange sneakers.

His phone stayed silent.

He drank more coffee and stared at the stupid phone. *Ping already, dammit.*

Nothing. He went up to the counter for the first refill of caffeine—and heard the ping from there.

He would have rushed back to the table but he didn't want hot coffee sloshing all over his hand.

I care about this woman a little too much, he realized.

He sat and picked up his phone and read her text.

My mom let me know Gram and Great-Gram are back on their feet, so I texted my mom and crew to meet me and Danny for breakfast at the caf in fifteen minutes. I'm going to tell them the truth.

You can make me the heavy, he texted. Tell them I ended the engagement.

Nah. My sister will feel awful about getting married this coming weekend in that case. What's that wise saying? The truth shall set me free? Everyone will be mad for one second, then forget it and focus on the real bride—Evie. That's my hope anyway.

Mad for one second? That crew? Ha. Her mother and aunt had been mad at each other for months.

I'll be thinking of you, he texted.

She didn't respond to that one.

He sure hoped his breakfast would be ready soon. He needed to be out of here before Sadie and her family arrived. Luckily, a minute later, Fran called out his ticket number in her booming voice, always good when there was a crowd here, and he got his tray. Mmm, the pancakes and bacon looked and smelled amazing.

He sat and drizzled maple syrup on the pancakes, but after taking all of three bites, Sadie, Danny and family came in—sister, mother, aunt, grandmother and great-grandmother. Everyone was chatting and happy so she clearly hadn't told them yet. He got it—she didn't want to ruin their appetites.

Sixty-year-old Cowboy Joe, who never took off his Stetson, came out from the kitchen making peekaboo faces at Danny. "Peekaboo, I see you!" Joe said, covering and uncovering his face.

"Dada!" Danny said, reaching for Cowboy Joe with a big smile.

Axel's mouth dropped open. He glanced over at Sadie and hers had done the same.

Cowboy Joe grinned and took Danny, hoisting him high in the air. Danny gave his grizzled brown-gray beard a yank.

Vanessa laughed. "He's been calling every man with dark hair Dada since we got here. Couple of days ago he called out to a ranch hand who couldn't be more than twenty, and the guy almost fainted."

Sadie's face brightened. She looked at Axel, who gave her a "phew" smile and she smiled back.

It was a phase. A toddler phase. Calling men *Dada*. Danny had a mama and applied that to only Sadie but he didn't have a dada so all men were that.

You're not special to him, after all, Axel told himself, but suddenly his pancakes were turning into cement in his stomach. What the hell was this? Wasn't he supposed to be elated that he wasn't special? That he wasn't anyone's dada?

False alarm, he texted Sadie. He could hear her phone ping. He watched her reach for her phone and read the text. She glanced at him.

I should still tell, she texted back.

Let Evie be. Let Izzy have this time. Let your mother be overjoyed. You'll fix it when you get home. You'll tell them I ended the engagement, that I couldn't commit after all, and everything will be fine—no one will be mad at you that way.

Except she didn't *look* fine as she read the words.

And he didn't *feel* fine.

Sigh. He really didn't know what the heck was going on with him. Or her. Or them.

"Why is your handsome groom-to-be sitting all by his lonesome?" Izzy asked after placing her order for scrambled eggs and toast. She didn't wait for an answer as she made her way slowly to his table with her red cane.

Sadie watched as Axel stood and took her great-grandmother's arm. Izzy leaned forward to offer her cheek for a kiss, and Axel obliged with a warm smile, then helped her into a chair. Sadie's heart physically moved in her chest, and she put her hand over the spot. My word, did she love this man.

Oh, God. She really did love him.

Once the whole group was seated and awaiting their tickets to be called, Axel stood behind Sadie and put his hands on her shoulders. How could someone so anti-marriage be so good at this faux engagement? He was ridiculously believable as her fiancé.

"Pick you up at four to head into town, Sadie?" he asked.

For a second she had no idea what he was talking about. Until she'd walked here and Danny had called Cowboy Joe *Dada*, she'd thought she was going to come clean to her family during breakfast, just blurt it out, rip off the Band-Aid. That and her time with Axel at an end had made her miserable last night, and she'd thought of little else. But now that she felt better about the Dada thing—clearly a phase—she didn't feel so panicked. What he'd texted made sense to her, and yeah, gave her a huge out, and she thought he was right. Let her family have this week instead of making everyone upset and uncomfortable—especially Evie after all her sister had opened up about. Viv had three wedding-related meetings set up for Evie this morning. Evie, Sadie, Viv and Tabby were all going. That was another thing Sadie didn't want to mess up—if Tabby was coming, that meant the two elder sisters had at least talked to declare another temporary truce for the week.

The afternoon meeting was about the letter from his father, she realized—the list of addresses. Sadie was so curious. One coincidental visit to Manuela's and he'd learned so much about his parents—particularly his father. Some very nice things. Things that had actually gotten him thinking. Let him open that letter after almost nine months.

She liked his hands on her shoulders. The warm weight of them was comforting—and a nice touch.

"Danny and I will be there," Sadie said. She'd be spending the day with her family and could feel the relief radiating that she wouldn't have to tell them the truth about her and Axel just yet.

Not that she was happy about it. Saying Axel had dumped her once they got home would be adding another lie to the mix. But then again, it would finally be over, just like *they'd* be over, and she would be heartbroken and could use the familial support and boxes of Puffs tissues and Ben & Jerry's. That heartache would not be fake.

"Danny, too?" her mom asked. "Why don't you let me and Great-Gram and Great-Great-Gram take our precious boy today. We barely got to see him the last two days, didn't we," she said, giving her grandson, beside her in a high chair, a soft tap on the nose.

Danny giggled. "Gram. Gray-Gram. More Gray-Gram!" He couldn't say "great-gram" and referred to Vanessa as "gray-gram" and Izzy as "more gray-gram." The family cracked up every time he said it. Only Izzy actually had gray hair since his gray-gram Vanessa kept hers an ash blond.

"And Gray-Aunt Tabby," Sadie's aunt put in, staring down Viv.

Good for you, Tab, Sadie thought. She narrowed her eyes at her mother. Tabby was fierce in staking her claim on spending time with her family, whether wedding-related or enjoying the ranch. *Don't you dare tell her no when you already agreed she was joining*, Sadie yelled in her head.

Viv lifted her chin but didn't say anything, which meant a huffy *fine*. Luckily, their order tickets were called and everyone stopped talking.

"Allow me," Axel said, bringing over two trays at a time until everyone was served.

Could the man be more gallant? She had chosen her faux fiancé well.

"Any*hoo*," Viv said, cutting into her cheese omelet, "Sadie and Axel, you two go off and wedding plan or whatever you're doing in Bear Ridge at four o'clock. We're happy to have our darling boy for as long as you need."

Sadie sipped her coffee. "Thanks, all of you. He sure is getting lots of great family time this week."

She'd miss her son—and she always felt like something wasn't quite right in the world when she was away from Danny—but she knew it was good for her relatives and for Danny to spend a lot of time together. Back home, during the week, Danny went to the excellent day care at work for hospital employees, and she got to stop in several times a day to see him. She always had lunch with him. Her mom would be retiring from her own job as a librarian later this year and she said she wanted to watch Danny full-time until he started preschool. Sadie liked that he was getting this early exposure to different kids and adults, but it would be nice for his grandmother and great-grandmother and great-great-grandmother to spend time with him.

"Well, see you later, then, Sadie. Bye, all," Axel said. He smiled and waved and then was gone.

"Such a handsome one!" Izzy said with a twinkle in her eyes.

"And such a gentleman!" Vanessa said. "Like my daddy was."

Aw, Sadie wished her great-grandfather could be here with them but he'd passed away four years ago. The male relatives, including Sadie's dad and grandpa, were spending a lot of time fishing and riding horses, neither of which Sadie's crew was interested in. Viv and Vanessa always thought of the family reunions as "girl time" since they got "quite enough" of their husbands at home.

Izzy gave a firm nod. "Got that right."

That got breakfast off to a good start, so they turned their attention to eating and complimenting their entrées and the coffee. When everyone was done, Sadie dropped Danny off with her cousin, Vanessa and Izzy went to wilderness yoga for seniors, and Sadie and her sister, mom and aunt got in Evie's car for a trip to Prairie City, where Viv had made appointments at a florist, a caterer and a party store that had everything from Halloween costumes to elegant candlesticks.

Evie wanted a rustic-elegant simple wedding for her and Marshall's eighty-two guests. According to her long chat the other day with Daisy Dawson, who'd organized a few weddings at the ranch so far, thirteen centerpieces were all they'd need to doll up the ballroom on the second floor of the ranch's lodge. The grand white building, which had been recently built, had been made to look antique.

There were arched floor-to-ceiling windows across one entire wall, a gorgeous chandelier, a polished wood dance floor and a large deck that would be festooned with white lights. Evie explained how the room would be arranged for the reception. The ceremony itself would be held outside behind the lodge, and the ranch would provide the arbor, red carpet to create the aisle and chairs. The weather for Saturday evening was supposed to be low seventies and not a drop of rain in the forecast. The reception would be in the lovely ballroom and spill onto the stone deck.

"That all sounds absolutely perfect," Aunt Tabby said as Evie drove down the service road that led to the freeway. "I never got married, of course, but if I had, I would have wanted the wedding you're planning."

"Did you just never fall in love?" Evie asked—daringly since their mom had always told her daughters that Tabby Winston viewed her singlehood as a failure that she didn't like to talk about.

Tabby didn't respond right away. "Actually, I did fall in love. With a wonderful guy and he proposed." She glanced out the window as though it was still painful for her. Sadie's heart went out to her aunt. She'd never heard this story before.

"Oh no," Evie said. "Please don't tell me he left you at the altar."

"Worse," Tabby said, tucking her auburn hair behind her ears.

"What could be worse?" Sadie asked, thinking of how she'd overheard that the father of Daisy Dawson's baby had left her at the altar when she was nine months pregnant. A guest had happened by and helped deliver little Tony right on the side of the road—and now they were married.

"I left *him* at the altar," Tabby said, shaking her head. "What an idiot I was."

"Don't beat yourself up," Viv told her, turning slightly to look at her sister in the back seat. "You did what felt right at the time. That's all you can do." Clearly, Viv knew all about this, and that made sense, since the sisters had always been so close.

Sadie looked at her mom in the passenger seat. That had been kind of Viv to say. Maybe there was hope here after all.

"I guess," Tabby said. And it was clear that Viv and Tabby had talked a lot about the subject over the years.

Evie pulled over onto the shoulder of the road and put the car in Park. "Wait a minute." She turned around to face her aunt. "You called off the wedding at the last minute? What happened?"

Tabby sighed. "Some other guy turned my head around and made me think *he* was the real one, the real Mr. Right. He swept me off my feet, and suddenly I thought I'd found the man I was truly meant to spend my life with. And ooh boy, was your gram mad at me. She thought I was nuts to throw away a good man for a whirlwind romance. I was so in love, though, and no one could tell me anything. But—"

Uh-oh.

"He dumped me after three weeks," Tabby continued. "I realized what a horrible fool I'd been, but my fiancé wouldn't take me back. I don't blame him. He married someone else six months later. Kudos to your gram for not once saying I told you so. You, too, Vivvy."

Viv leaned over and put a hand on her sister's arm. That was nice to hear, that Viv had been there for Tabby—and that Tabby remembered and brought it up. That was the kind of thing that cemented a relationship, that had to matter more than a silly argument.

Sadie gave her aunt's hand a squeeze. "I'm so sorry, Aunt Tabby."

"Didn't you start dating eventually, though?" Evie asked, pulling onto the road since their appointment was in fifteen minutes with the caterer.

"I did, but I never fell for anyone again. I liked some of the guys very much, tried to love some over the years, but I couldn't imagine marrying any of them. And I must have gone on a thousand dates since then. Here I am, still single."

"Eh, not everyone has to get married or have kids," Viv said. "You've had a fun and interesting life. You have a career, you have a big family you help out with, you travel, you volunteer. Girls, did you know your aunt Tabby volunteers at the NICU twice a week? The sickest babies, too."

Sadie knew Tabby volunteered at the hospital because she'd run into her there a few times, but she didn't know about the NICU. Her aunt had always said she was on a rotation of departments.

"Well, I missed out on the chance to have a baby of my own, so I figured I'd help out with those sweet infants," Tabby said. "And besides, I hope I've been more than just Aunt Tabby to you two girls. You know you're like daughters to me."

"We know, Tabs," Evie said, reaching her right arm out to rub Tabby's shoulder.

"We certainly do," Sadie added. Tabby had always been like a second mom to her and Evie. The older she got, the more Sadie realized how careful Tabby had been not to overstep on their mother's ways and style when it came to her nieces, even when Tabby thought Viv was dead wrong about something. They were lucky to have her.

If Aunt Tabby wanted a boyfriend or a husband she could certainly get out there and find herself one. She was lovely and vibrant.

"Do you all want to know a secret I've been keeping?" Tabby asked with a shy smile. Tabby was never shy about anything. So what was *this* about?

Viv turned around. "Now you're keeping secrets, too?" she snapped.

"What's that supposed to mean?" Tabby asked.

Viv glared at her sister. "We said we'd try to put aside our issues for the sake of the reunion. But now you have a secret from me?"

Oh, Mom, Sadie thought. *Why are you so dramatic?* Viv was the older sister and could be a lot less mature than Tabby.

"Well, we haven't exactly been talking," Tabby pointed out, her hazel eyes flashing.

"Your fault as well as mine," Viv insisted, crossing her arms over her chest, her signature move. "But a secret warrants talking!"

"Fine," Tabby said. "I'll tell you now. I have a date tonight."

Viv's mouth dropped open, and the energy in the air instantly changed from tense to pure curiosity. "A date with who?"

"Cowboy Joe," Viv said. "That handsome devil who runs the ranch kitchen in the caf. He's a widower and asked me out, and I said yes."

Sadie burst into a grin. Cowboy Joe was around sixty, she thought, tall and rangy with a full head of gray-black hair, a grizzled beard and squinting brown eyes. He reminded her of the actor Sam Elliott. Apparently, he'd been the chef at the ranch when Axel's grandparents had owned it, but he'd had to leave when Axel's dad ran the place into the ground. Noah Dawson had rehired him once he rebuilt, and Cowboy Joe had said he loved being "back home."

Sadie couldn't stop smiling. "That's great! He's quite handsome. Looks like a real cowboy."

"And he's so charming and nice," Evie said. "Did you see the way Danny ran right to him in the cafeteria and Joe picked him up and played peekaboo with him? He's a doll."

"You could have told me you were looking to date," Viv said. "I would have set you up with my endodontist—he's divorced and looking."

"He's my endodontist, too, and has bad breath," Tabby pointed out.

"Ew," Evie said, shaking her head and grimacing in the rearview mirror.

Sadie laughed. "Where are you guys going on the date?"

"Joe is taking me into Bear Ridge to a steakhouse that has a dance floor. You know how I love to dance."

"Well," Viv said, "do you want my opinion, not that you asked?"

Sadie rolled her eyes. Her mother was too much sometimes.

"Sure," Tabby said, clearly bracing herself for judgy Vivian.

Viv lifted her chin. "I think Cowboy Joe is a real catch and that your date sounds wonderful."

And sometimes Sadie's mother was just right. *Go, Mom.*

Tabby grinned. "I wonder if he'll try to kiss me. I hope so. He's been widowed for three years. He said he hasn't done much dating but there was something about me." She was beaming.

Sadie was so happy for her aunt. If only Axel Dawson would feel that way about Sadie—that there was something about *her* and fall madly in love…

"We're here!" Evie said, pulling into the little parking lot behind Calista's Catering.

Now Sadie would spend hours helping her sister plan a wedding she wished were her own—with a groom who never would be. At least Sadie was still faux-engaged, she thought, not that it really helped.

Chapter Eleven

"So what happens when the Winstons leave on Sunday?" Noah asked in the big barn after the staff meeting.

Axel kept his focus on straightening out the tack area, despite its being perfectly tidy and the ranch hands' job. "What do you mean?"

"He *means*," Daisy said as she tightened her long ponytail, "are you and Sadie going to keep up the pretend engagement, or are you going to break up?"

Actually, Axel knew what Noah had meant but was procrastinating answering. The sun caught on both his siblings' wedding rings, and Axel found himself staring at the gold bands. Even Noah, who'd been a wild child, had settled down and had never been happier. That had caught Axel by surprise. But Axel had never been a wild type, except for the lone wolf part. He did like sitting out on mountain ledges and taking in the panoramic views of such natural beauty and quiet and perfection. Lately, though, when he felt he needed one of those ledge sits, he kept envisioning Sadie beside him. A little conversation, a little silence. Just having her there, next to him.

"Sadie will tell her family that I ended the engagement, that I couldn't commit after all," Axel explained. "Everyone stays happy this week and once home, Sadie can save face."

"Oh, propose to her for real already," Daisy said. "Then you'll be happy, too."

Axel's eyes almost popped. "Excuse me? *What?*"

"I see how you look at Sadie," Daisy explained. "How you treat Danny. That's not pretend, Axel."

Noah looked at his sister, then at Axel. "You know, last night Sara asked me if you and Sadie were the real thing now, Ax. She said the two of you seemed truly in love."

Axel frowned. "It's called *acting.*"

"You were never in a school play for a reason," Daisy pointed out. "And you're the worst liar."

"Then how do I have y'all fooled?" he asked, wanting this conversation over.

Daisy chuckled—dryly. "Maybe you don't. Maybe you really have fallen for Sadie Winston."

Axel shook his head. "I'm not looking for a real relationship, Daize. I know you want me settled down with a family, but that's not me. I'm on my own and fine that way."

He knew Daisy's master plan when he'd first come back to the ranch three months ago had been to get him settled here. She'd been trying to fix him up so he'd fall in love and stay put, build a cabin on the property. Well, she'd gotten part of her grand plan—he'd built the home on the ranch—but he hadn't fallen in love. He wouldn't let himself. Because he knew what happened the last time he'd let his heart be the boss. He'd gotten run over by a tractor, twice. Once for the woman who'd left him. Once for her baby girl whom he'd never seen again. *You don't love, you don't lose.* It was that simple and really, someone should embroider that on a pillow.

"Gotta take him at his word," Noah said, shrugging at Daisy. But Axel caught the little smile passed between the two. Harrumph.

"Anyhoo," he said, using his faux mother-in-law-to-be's favorite way to change subjects. "Guess where I'm headed this afternoon."

"Did you just say anyhoo?" Noah asked, peering at him. He put his hand to Axel's forehead as if to feel for fever.

Daisy laughed. "Fine. We can change the subject, Avoider Axel. Where ya headed?"

Axel took the folded letter from his pocket. "This is the letter Dad left for me." He handed the piece of paper with the four addresses to Noah. He'd already spoken to Daisy about the list.

"What's the one on Main Street?" Noah asked, narrowing his eyes as if trying to place it around his favorite places in town—the coffee shop, a fish and chips place he and Sara frequented.

"Manuela's Mexican Café," he said. "Turns out that's where Dad met my mom."

Noah nodded. "He's definitely trying to tell you a story with these addresses. I wonder what the other places are. You recognize any, Daisy?"

She looked over his shoulder. "Hey, 22 Colby Way—I know what that is. It's Gram and Gramps's old house. Before they bought this land and built the ranch. Dad grew up there till he was five or six, I think."

"Yeah?" Axel asked, eyeing the address. "Maybe I'll check that out first."

Noah looked at the list again. "I don't recognize the others. Hurley Lane is a private road with one big ranch on it. An older couple lives there, I think. Not sure what Dad's connection to the Hurleys was."

Well, that was helpful, actually. Axel didn't like the unknown, and now three of the four addresses were accounted for and one could be crossed off— Manuela's. He reclaimed the list and returned it to the envelope and his pocket.

"Why would he send me to Gram and Gramps's old house?" Axel asked. "They moved out of there over fifty years ago."

"He must have had a good reason," Daisy said. "Want company there?"

Axel swallowed. He was going to get it for this. "I appreciate that, but, uh, Sadie's coming with me. We're leaving at four. I think I'll start with the old Dawson place and see what I can find out."

"Interesting," Daisy said, a twinkle in her blue eyes. "Sadie, your fake fiancée, is going with you on this personal mission. Away from the ranch and her relatives, the ones you need to play house for."

"We're…" Axel began, then clamped his mouth shut. They were what? Friends? He supposed he'd been about to say that but he and Sadie were more than friends. Friends didn't kiss the way they had—two times. Friends didn't have the intensity of attraction that they had.

"Let us know what you find out, will you?" Noah asked. "I'm curious why he's sending you to these places. Must be some things he wants you to find out."

Axel nodded. "Will do."

Noah and Daisy finally left, again giving each other a knowing look that had him inwardly groaning.

Axel stared at the hay bales, trying to get his brain back on the ranch, on his day. He had a busy one, leading two wilderness tours, patrolling a beginner's horseback riding program and helping the hands mend a section of fence. Then at four, he'd meet Sadie and go into the great unknown, where he kind of felt he was already.

"So what's your dream wedding?" Evie asked as she and Sadie both flopped on their beds in the cabin. Today had been a long but fun day of tastings, choosing flowers and buying centerpieces. Evie had already booked friends of Marshall's as the band: the Hell Yeahs. They were alternative country-rock who did amazing covers of all of Evie's and Marshall's favorite songs. "Ugh, that was a dumb question, sorry," she added with a grimace, turning on her side to face Sadie. "You probably made your dream wedding when you got married the first time."

Sadie smiled. "Are you kidding? That was more *Mom's* dream wedding."

Evie laughed. "Yeah, I do remember her saying to you, 'You want a poufy princess dress, *right*? You want filet mignon in béarnaise sauce, *right*?

Your bridesmaids are all wearing the same dress, *right*?'"

"I wasn't into wedding planning and Mom was, so I just said 'right' to everything unless it was truly awful. À la, 'You will aim your bouquet only for Evie or Tabby, who I will strategically place together. Strongest catcher wins, right?'"

"Ugh, thanks for saving me from that." Evie giggled. "I'll never forget Izzy catching the bouquet on her lap in her wheelchair and saying, 'Well, I *am* single.'" Evie cracked up.

Sadie laughed. "If I'd been into planning, I would have created a wedding like yours. Elegant yet simple. Pink and white flowers. White lights. A great band and great food."

"Simple works especially when you've got the highlight in the groom," Evie said. "I can't wait to say I do and kiss my husband and be a team. A whole new life is awaiting me—that's how it feels. I'd love to get pregnant right away. I hope I do."

Sadie smiled and turned on her side. "You're so lucky," she said and the wistfulness in her voice made her remember she was supposedly just as lucky.

"Maybe you and Axel can get married in the lodge, too," Evie said.

Sadie was lucky, too, because just then, their mom poked her head in their room and this stab-in-the-heart conversation was cut short. Danny was in her arms, a piece of what looked like a cider doughnut, his favorite, in his hand. The big smile on his face said Mommy was right about that. "Guess what Tabby's date for tonight had a ranch hand send over to our cabin?" Viv asked. "Oh, just a big box of two dozen freshly baked doughnuts of every kind imaginable. Come and get 'em before I eat all the cream-filled ones. You know you love those, Sadie. Hurry before Axey gets here. It's almost four."

Axey. Now he had a nickname? Sadie sighed and pulled herself up by the bedpost.

"Tell Izzy to leave me a powdered jelly!" Evie said.

"Oops!" Izzy called out. "How about half of one?" Sadie could hear Izzy chuckling from the living room.

She smiled. Saved by doughnuts. And Aunt Tabby's new romance. She was glad some people were having real affairs of the heart even if hers was fakety-fake.

Their destination, 22 Colby Way, was a tiny yellow house down a dirt road. A white farmhouse was about a quarter mile beyond and Axel figured the yellow house had been the hands' quarters at one time.

"I guess this was their starter home when my grandmother and grandfather were newlyweds,"

Axel said. "Doesn't look like it could fit more than two people."

Sadie stared up at the lemon yellow house with white trim. "It looks sweet and cozy. So what's the plan? Knock?"

"I guess."

They got out and walked up the two steps to the stoop. He'd been right to invite Sadie to join him. He wouldn't want to be here alone. Axel pressed the doorbell and a young woman came to the door.

"Hi," Axel said. "I recently found out that my grandparents used to own this house and I thought I'd come take a look if that's all right. I understand if it's intrusive."

The woman peered at him. "Are you a Dawson?"

Axel nodded. "How'd you know?" Maybe she'd known his father.

"Well, my grandparents owned this house for like the last fifty years. They retired and sold it to my husband and me. I know they bought it from the Dawsons, who ran the dude ranch before it went south."

Axel smiled. "It's north again. It's completely rebuilt and reopened."

"Oh, that's good to know. Well, come in. I'll show you around. The house is tiny so there's not much to see."

There was a little kitchen with barely room for

a two-person round table. Square living room. A very small dining room. A bathroom. The woman led them upstairs. "Two bedrooms up here. And the attic. But that's full of old furniture and my family's keepsakes, like old report cards."

Axel glanced around. Not much to see. He followed the woman downstairs, Sadie trailing. He wondered why his dad had bothered putting this place on the list. Fifty years was a long time. Maybe because Bo Dawson had lived here as a kid and he remembered it?

"Could we look out back?" Axel asked, peering out the window at the long but narrow backyard. There was a line of trees at the edge of the yard and a rickety tree house of sorts.

"Sure," she said. "Take your time. Oh—definitely go up in the tree house. The walls are covered in framed kitschy photos of who knows what. I think some of it might have been there when my grandparents bought the house. They loved the tree house and kept adding to what was already on the walls."

Axel and Sadie went outside and walked to the edge of the yard. Nothing to see here either. He shrugged. "Not much of a story."

"How old was your dad when your grandparents sold the house?" Sadie asked.

"Ten, I think."

"Well, maybe this counted as home to him and he wanted you to see it for yourself."

"I guess. Let's check out the tree house."

There were seven steps up and Axel tested the bottom rung—very sturdy. The tree house was built rock-solid—more like a cabin than the usual kiddie play structure. He wondered if his grandparents had built the tree house or if the other owners had. He climbed up, and since it was sturdy he went to the top and motioned Sadie up. There was a door that swung in, two windows and a braided rug in the middle of the dusty floor. No one had been up here in a while, it seemed. The walls were indeed covered, practically every available spot, with framed pictures of all kinds. One was an old rodeo advertisement from the '50s. Another was a Wyoming Wildcats team photo from the '90s. There were lots of framed local ads of livestock auctions and bull riders.

Axel drew closer to another one, a handwritten list, it looked like, in a gold frame.

My rules for life.

By Bo Dawson, age 10 and a half.

Axel sucked in a breath. "Sadie, come look at this."

She gasped. "They kept this up here for fifty years?"

"Well, the tree house is full of memorabilia, either theirs or my grandparents' or a mix. Like the woman said, I guess her grandparents liked it as it was and kept it."

"Well, now we know why this place was on the list. Because it was home and maybe he knew the tree house was left alone. Maybe he'd stopped by as an adult."

Axel stepped close and read the list his father had made.

My rules for life.
by Bo Dawson, age 10 and a half.

1. Try to do the right thing even if you don't want to. I only want to half the time.

2. Say sorry only if you mean it.

3. Your parents think they know everything but they probably do.

4. I wish we had money.

5. Someday I'm gonna have everything I want. I might even be president.

6. Birthdays are big deals and you should get everything on your list.

7. Everyone should have a dog. It's not fair I don't have one.

8. I'm good at math but not good at spelling or reading fast and I don't care.

9. There's no such thing as ghosts.

10. I wish I had a brother. If I ever have a family, I'm gonna have ten kids.

Axel stood there, speechless, oddly moved by the eclectic list. He loved having a piece of his father as a ten-year-old, so sure of himself.

"Six kids probably felt like ten," Sadie said with a smile.

Axel turned to her. "No doubt." He turned back to the list. "He loved Dude. Any time I'd bring the dog by, my dad would make such a fuss over him, get right on the ground and scratch him all over. One time he told me to wait a second, then came from the house with a chew toy he said he'd bought for the next time he saw Dude."

"Your dad definitely had his good side, Axel."

He nodded. "People are complicated. As I said before, it's so much easier if things are black-and-white. Either-or. Good and bad."

She reached for his hand and held it, and he squeezed it, then let go. This was too…personal, intimate, close, and the air started slowly disappearing from his lungs.

"Do you want to ask if you can have this?" Sadie suggested.

He took out his phone and stood back and snapped a photo of it. "I think it belongs here. Fifty years and counting."

"I'm surprised your grandparents didn't take it to the new house and hang it in his room or something."

He looked at the list again, his dad's handwriting as a ten-year-old not too far off from his adult handwriting. "Maybe they thought it belonged here with this chapter of their life. You know what I mean? Like, this is who Bo was when he lived in this house."

She smiled. "I can see that. And maybe the tree house walls were full of photos when your grandparents bought it and they kept the tradition by adding to it and leaving it. The new owners certainly didn't remove anything in fifty years."

He slowly turned, taking in all the stuff, imagining his dad here as a kid, lying on the rug, staring at the pictures, dreaming of the future. The thought made him smile. "I'm ready to go," he said.

Sadie climbed down first and he followed. The owner of the house happened to be watering flowers in the backyard, so Axel waved and called out thanks as they headed to the street where his car was parked.

He opened Sadie's door for her, then got in himself, his chest seizing on him. His father was once a kid making lists about his rules for life. How had that firecracker of a boy let his life unravel, especially when he had so much? The ranch, wives who loved him, six children who needed him.

"You okay?" Sadie asked once they were buckled up.

"I don't know why hearing about his life hits me so hard," Axel said, staring out the windshield. "He was an addict—to gambling and alcohol—and couldn't help himself. I know that—intellectually. But here—" he slapped a hand on the left side of his chest "—I'm just so…" He let it go. What was the point?

"Angry. Hurt," Sadie finished for him.

He turned to her. "Yeah, those."

"Want to visit another address or was this enough for one day?" she asked.

"This was more than enough." He shook his head. "Done in by a silly list written by my dad as a kid. What the hell is wrong with me?"

"You're human. And it's incredibly painful all you're dealing with, Axel. You once said you felt like his death was your fault."

He sucked in a breath. "I should have dragged him to rehab. They would have done a physical and found that he was dying."

"You didn't know. That doesn't make losing him your fault," she said gently. "How'd you get the news?"

He turned to her, surprised she'd asked. Most people would want to change the heavy subject. Not Sadie. "I was far out on a cliff on a search and rescue job and a chopper picked me up to take me to the hospital. Noah had found him barely conscious on the couch. He realized Bo was truly in trouble and called 911. I made it to his bedside five minutes before he passed away."

"Oh, Axel."

"All six of us got there in time. One of the last things my father said was, *You're all here.* And he said it with tears in his eyes and such surprise on his face. He left this world knowing that no matter what, we cared, we were there for him."

"I'm so glad for that. For him and for all of you."

"Me, too," Axel whispered.

She leaned over and pulled him to her and he wrapped his arms around her, the embrace, the scent of her, the softness of her so comforting.

"Thanks for being here," he said. "I owe you one."

She laughed. "Uh, I owe you a week's worth, so trust me, I still owe *you*." She looked at him and shifted in her seat. "Let's head to the cabin. I'll make you some comfort food."

"Home-cooked meal? Sounds good to me."

The thought of Sadie in his house, sharing a meal with her, just the two of them cocooned, sounded better than good. It sounded *necessary*.

Chapter Twelve

Sadie looked through the cabinets in Axel's kitchen and the fridge, and once decided on her menu, she took out the ingredients. At first, she thought she'd make his favorite, baked ziti, but he'd had that last night *and* he was out of both ziti and penne. But he had pizza dough and marinara sauce and mozzarella cheese, which meant yummy, gooey pizza.

I sure do feel at home here, she thought, spreading the sauce and generously laying on the cheese. She slid the pizza into the oven and set the timer, imagining herself living here, she and Axel taking turns making dinner, Sadie coming home from work at the hospital to a warm, cozy, luxe cabin with spaghetti and meatballs on the burners, garlic bread in the oven, *their* dog, Dude, excited to see her and Danny.

A few steps ahead of yourself, girl, she warned herself, but she loved the pictures in her head and refused to blink them away. *Axel coming down the stairs with just a towel wrapped around his sexy hips, kissing her hello, the towel dropping...*

Okay, now she was truly carried away. Although he had gone upstairs to take a shower, to erase the day, and it *was* possible he'd come down in just a teeny towel tied loosely around his hips, hair dripping onto his naked chest... Unlikely but still possible.

Except she knew Axel and he'd never do that, despite her wishing he would.

Back to reality. Which meant checking in with her mom to see how Danny was.

He's happy as can be, her mom texted back. We're at the petting zoo. Don't rush—we're about to head to dinner in the caf and I'll get Danny to bed on time and give him a kiss from you and Axey.

Again with the Axey.

Just in case she wouldn't be back before Danny's bedtime, she FaceTimed her mother so she could see Danny and tell him she loved him. "'Oats funny!"

Danny said, and when they disconnected, her sister sent her an adorable shot of Danny feeding hay to a little white goat.

"Something smells amazing," Axel said, coming downstairs with damp tousled hair—almost like in her minifantasy. Ooh la la. He was beyond sexy in his faded jeans, navy T-shirt and bare feet. He smelled like shampoo and soap—even more delicious than the scent of pizza.

"It's a surprise," she said. "But it's definitely comfort food."

"Can't wait. And after dinner, I thought we'd play that So You Think You Know Your Significant Other? game."

She gaped at him. "Really?"

He laughed. "No. I am *completely* joking."

"Thought so," she said with a knowing nod, then peered in the oven. The cheese was bubbling. Five minutes and the pizza would be done.

"Glass of red wine?" he asked. "Daisy gave me a bottle called Dancing Alpacas for doing her a favor last weekend. I can't promise it'll be good. Do you think our alpacas break out into the Macarena when we're all not looking?"

She laughed. "Maybe the chicken dance. And I'd love a glass." Wine, pizza and handsome, sexy Axel. It was almost too much.

The bottle featured an upright brown-and-white

alpaca with his hooves in the air. She smiled as he poured two glasses.

He handed her one, then held up his. "To us getting through a trying week together."

Happy chills raced up her spine. "I will drink to that." What she wanted to say was that she was touched by his toast. The past days had been trying on lots of levels and they *were* going through it together. The faux engagement. The walk through his father's life.

I feel so close to you, she thought wistfully, unable to drag her eyes off him. His still-damp dark hair, the blue eyes, strong jawline and incredible shoulders, broad and strong.

She had to stop staring, so she took a sip of the dry, spicy wine, which sent a warm glowy boost where she needed it. "Not bad at all," she said, holding up the glass. "We can eat in the living room if you'd like, get comfy on the couch. Dinner is that kind."

"Oh good. Movie?"

Again, goose bumps. Dinner and a movie. She thought about her mom telling her not to rush. She and Axel could both use a relaxing night, a little escape into a movie.

He sipped his wine and gave a "not bad" nod, then flicked on the big-screen TV and rolled through the guide. "There it is. No need for anything else if *The Princess Bride* is on."

She grinned. "I totally agree. And I haven't seen it in years." Those happy chills were back, breaking into goose bumps on her arms. This felt like a date.

It is a date. Whether he likes it or not, and who knows, maybe he does like it. Maybe Mr. Marriage Squeezes the Air Out of My Lungs is falling for me as hard as I'm falling for him, and who can stop the progress of true love? Not even Prince Humperdinck.

While Axel set the coffee table, Sadie made a simple salad and tossed it with creamy Italian dressing.

"Be right back," Axel said and went out the kitchen door into the yard, which confused her because he didn't bring Dude, who'd already gone out when they'd returned. When he came in a few minutes later with a bouquet of wildflowers, she went completely still, the air squeezed out of *her* lungs.

This *was* a date.

He smiled at her, and everything inside got the warm fuzzies and not from the wine. She watched him grab a vase off the mantel and fill it with water and then put in the flowers. He set the vase on the big coffee table. "Dude," he said to the dog, who sat on the side of the table, gnawing at a rawhide, "when a woman cooks for you, you bring her flowers, even if they're from the yard."

"Wildflowers are the best kind," she said, the warm fuzzies getting hotter.

Ooh, boy, did she want to kiss him. Run her hands along his broad shoulders, across his back, in his hair. The oven timer dinged, jolting her out of her little dream.

"You sit and enjoy your wine," he said. "I'll get the pizza."

She did as he said, leaning back on the comfortable cushion. When was the last time she had a night like this that didn't involve someone she was related to or a colleague from work during their monthly movie nights in the hospital basement?

Within a half hour, the salad was almost gone, the pizza only crumbs and the bottle of Dancing Alpacas wine consumed. She and Axel were laughing and calling out famous lines from *The Princess Bride* as they watched, both declaring it in their top ten favorites of all time. And then the movie was over and she leaned her head against his shoulder—without thinking, just *feeling*.

He didn't stiffen. Or flinch.

Instead, he turned and lifted his hands to either side of her face. "I want to kiss you more than anything in the world right now."

"But will you still want to kiss me to-mor-rohhh?" she sang, her lips a mere inch from his. That was the issue. She wasn't so sure he *would* want to. He'd made himself so clear on the subject of a romantic relationship. This would not be going anywhere.

"I'll never stop wanting to kiss you, Sadie."

Oh, my. She could let herself have this. Tonight. Maybe she could get him out of her system that way. *Yeah right*, she thought. *Like that will happen. Stop rationalizing. If you let this happen, be prepared to accept what* will *happen—tomorrow morning.* She was going to have her heart handed to her either way.

She leaned forward and touched her lips to his and that was that. He kissed her so passionately her toes truly curled. Then his hands and lips were all over her, her mouth, her neck, her breastbone. He lifted her tank top to trail kisses across her stomach, and she flung the shirt off, watching his gaze move to her lacy pink bra—not the sexy one from the bridal boutique but plenty hot nonetheless. She peeled off his T-shirt, and his chest was everything she'd fantasized about. Muscled and hard. Every part of her body hummed and tingled and she gave completely in to the delicious sensations. She heard the zipper of her flippy yellow skirt being pulled down, and she reached for his zipper, eliciting a groan that sent shock waves through her.

And then they were naked, kissing, touching, feeling. She was kissing his neck when she saw one of his hands reaching for something on the coffee table—his wallet. She gasped inwardly, so

ready. Then she heard that telltale tear of a foil
packet and she resumed her trail of kisses along
his chest.

"Okay?" he whispered in her ear.

"Okay," she whispered back.

And then she lost all ability to process anything
but how good making love to Axel felt and how
completely in love with him she was.

Sadie woke up in the morning with a big smile
on her face, but it faded when she realized she was
alone in Axel's king-size bed. The door was closed
and she strained to listen for sounds—running
water or the clank of silverware; he could be taking a shower or making them breakfast. But there
was silence.

And then she saw the folded note with her name
on it propped against the lamp on the bedside table.

Yup. Gone. With the wind. The summer breeze.
I told you so, Sadie Winston!

Had it been worth it? Yes. Every amazing, I-am-
a-red-blooded-woman moment of it. It had been
a long time since she'd been with a man. Since
before her divorce. Her heart might feel a little
pushed around but her body felt rejuvenated and
alive and relaxed as if she'd gone to a yoga class
with her own attentive magic yogi.

But there was one part of her that felt all achy
and bruised. In her chest, to the left.

She'd been right to keep her expectations in check—not that that helped.

She grabbed the note and read it. *Morning. My brother needed my help so I had to leave early. Sleep in, relax, hang with Dude, whatever you like. Feel free to take the buggy home—I biked in. Talk to you later, Axel.*

Sigh. Sigh, sigh, sigh.

Feel free to take the buggy home. As in, leave at your leisure, but leave.

Well, come on, she *had* to leave. She was someone's mother, for heaven's sake. And she was at the ranch for her family reunion, not to luxuriate in her fake fiancé's bed all day. Even if she'd been invited to do that, which clearly she hadn't. He needed her gone when he returned and she knew it.

Ain't that romantic, she thought, lying down and pulling the covers up to her chin. He'd been honest from the start, though. He'd told her who he was. She'd let herself get caught up in the fantasy.

But last night had been so real—nothing about their wonderful evening had been fake. Their chemistry during dinner, their fun during the movie, the kiss that had led to much, much more. All very real, very honest emotions on both sides. She'd had an entire talk with herself about how things would likely be in the morning, hadn't she? She'd known this would happen, that Axel would not be beside her when she woke, feeding her red grapes.

Get up and go, she told herself. *Your life is elsewhere.*

A half hour later, showered and dressed, she went downstairs and into the kitchen to find the room spotless, even though they'd left it a complete mess last night. Axel had either gone down in the middle of the night or taken care of the kitchen before leaving this morning. The coffee maker was on and had at least two cups in it. She poured herself one and added cream and sugar, the hot brew helping.

She sighed for the fiftieth time and let Dude out and watched him sniff the grass and roll around in the sunshine. Back inside, she refilled his water bowl, though she was sure Axel had done that, then she gave him a pat before grabbing her purse and the key to the buggy, which he'd left on the counter next to the coffeepot with a big note: *Key to the buggy—leave it in the console. A.*

The man thought of everything—unfortunately. Because it meant he hadn't been there when she'd woken up for a reason. He hadn't wanted to be. Too much? Too intimate? Too much to say without being able to say anything because it was awkward?

She got in the buggy and drove to the big barn, parking on the side where he'd see it easily from any direction. She left the key, then got out and walked around the back of the barn where the horse stables were at the far end. Looking at the beautiful horses would cheer her up, get her ready to face the day and the truth.

"So have things evolved?" Sadie heard Daisy Dawson say from inside the barn.

"Evolved?" came Axel's voice.

Sadie stopped dead in her tracks and held her breath, flattening herself against the outside of the barn.

"With Sadie," Daisy said. "There's no way you're spending so much time together and nothing is happening. I see how you two look at each other!"

"Daisy, I keep telling you, I'm not in the market for anything right now. Can't you torment Rex or Zeke or Ford? They're the brothers you should be focused on—at least I'm *here*."

Torment? This line of questioning was *torment*? Asking about his feelings for her?

"Here but not here!" Daisy said, and Sadie wanted to clap like Meryl Streep and Jennifer Lopez had at the Oscars during Patricia Arquette's feminist acceptance speech.

Silence. Sadie could envision Axel throwing up his hands.

"You're so infuriating!" Daisy said. "Why do

you keep saying you're not ready for a real relationship? What does that even *mean*?"

"It's very clear, Daisy. Not ready. A wife, a child. I'm not ready."

"Not willing is more like it, supposedly older and wiser brother. If this is about coming from a broken home and having a negligent father, keep in mind that both Noah and I took to marriage and parenthood with flying colors and we all had the same dad. *You* determine who you want to be, not your past."

"I have work to do, Daisy," Axel said, his voice tinged with impatience.

Silence, and then, "Well, fine. Let the best thing that ever happened to you get away!"

Aw, that was kind of Daisy. Sadie wanted to rush in and hug her.

"Daize, I appreciate that you care. I really do. But this is my life, okay? Back off."

"You think this kind of love happens all the time, Axel? You should grab it and never let it go."

"Who said anything about love?" Axel said.

Sadie inwardly gasped, her heart clenching, and she staggered backward a bit. The pain in her chest almost knocked her to her knees.

Her "pep" talk in his cabin of you-knew-what-you-were-getting-into had clearly been rationalizing. Because hearing it like this—straight out after they'd slept together—was worse than she could have imagined.

Tears streaming down her cheeks, she ran to the stand of trees at the other side of the barn. She made sure no one was around and then wiped under her eyes and sucked in a breath and started walking.

She was surprised she could move at all with her heart breaking into pieces with each step.

She heard a gasp and turned and standing there staring at her was Daisy Dawson in her green Dawson Family Guest Ranch polo and a straw hat.

Oh no. Daisy walked up to her, peering at her as if trying to tell if Sadie had overheard that little conversation.

The red-rimmed eyes must have given that away.

"Sadie? Were you by any chance just over by the barn?"

Sadie nodded and felt her eyes well up again.

Daisy slung an arm around her shoulder. "I have the best chocolate-hazelnut coffee at my house. Want a cup or three?"

Sadie bit her lip. She turned around, curious if Axel had come out of the barn. Not that he'd necessarily know she'd overheard and that Daisy knew it; he could easily think they'd just happened to cross paths.

But he didn't come out of the barn. He was likely stewing.

Daisy was nice to offer to sit and talk with her, commiserate, tell Sadie her brother was a big fool, but Sadie had a feeling she'd feel worse. "I would love a cup, Daisy, but I'd better get back to the cabin. I miss Danny."

Daisy's blue eyes were sympathetic. "I know just what you mean. If I'm feeling bad, sometimes all I have to do is set eyes on Tony and the world rights itself."

Sadie smiled. "Exactly."

"I'm sorry you overheard that. Axel is…frustrating. But I'll bet he comes around."

Sadie wasn't sure what to say to that. She didn't want to wait and hope a man "came around." She wanted to be worth loving, plain and simple. And if Axel couldn't handle real emotions, real love, well, then he wasn't the man for her, was he?

Tough talk when she felt like she might crumble any second.

Ping.

A text from Axel: Can we talk?

Wow. The It's Not You It's Me conversation about to happen and so fast. Axel wanted to wipe his hands of what had happened last night, get them back on their "friendly" track.

Sadie held up her phone and showed Daisy, who smiled. "See, he's coming around already. I know my brother, Sadie. Don't give up on him." Daisy squeezed her hand and then headed toward the lodge.

I don't want to, Sadie thought. *But I know what I know.* Still, better to get this over with. There wasn't a lot of truth going around this week, so when a big bolt of it popped out, it could really knock someone upside the head.

Sadie texted back: Meet by the creek at the big rock? Now-ish?

See you in five.

She had no doubt what he was going to say. He was so sorry about last night, he shouldn't have let it happen, and in the light of day, he realized that he was still the same Axel he'd been the night of the bonfire, when he'd told her what marriage meant to him.

Sadie walked past her cabin, suddenly needing everyone in it to wrap her up in their support and love. Especially Izzy, who gave the best hugs and smelled like roses. But she kept going, also needing to brace herself for the conversation she was about to have.

And for the end of her and Axel. Maybe not the fake them. But the real them who had never had a chance.

Axel saw Sadie sitting on the big flat rock on the creek's bank, her back to him. The sight of her, even at quite a distance, caused a little stir in his chest. He was always happy to see Sadie. But he wasn't looking forward to this conversation. He wasn't sure what he wanted to say. To apologize for leaving her alone in his cabin this morning after the night they'd had, the most intimate physical experience two people could have.

When he'd woken up, Sadie spooned against him, he'd relished the feel of her so close to him, a new day with the woman who'd turned his life upside down and all around. But the more he lay there, the more that air-seeping feeling started working its way into his lungs, and when he got Noah's text, he'd felt relief. A reason to leave.

This shouldn't be complicated—*he* was making it complicated—but it was.

"Hey," he called out.

She turned around and didn't look too happy. She wore what she'd been wearing last night, and a barrage of memories hit him. Digging into that delicious pizza. Sharing the Dancing Alpacas wine. Watching *The Princess Bride* and shouting out lines of dialogue through most of it. Feeling so light and easy. Feeling so…close to her. So attracted. And the kiss, which had exploded into the best sex he'd ever had. More than just passionate.

Because you feel more for this woman than you want to deal with?

"Look," she said, staying seated but facing him.

"I'm going to be honest. I returned the buggy to the big barn and I happened to overhear your conversation with your sister. So everything you might want to say now? You already said it."

Oh hell. Punch to the gut.

Dammit. A lot of what he'd said came back to him. Echoing in his head.

Particularly: *Who said anything about love?*

He grimaced. "Daisy has a way of making me feel like a cornered wolf when she gets on the topic of my love life."

"You told me your position on serious relationships the first night of the reunion. I guess I was hoping I might have changed your mind, that I was special enough, that I meant enough to you for that to happen." She looked away, and he wanted nothing more than to pull her to him and hold her.

"You *are* special to me, Sadie. You and Danny both. But I have to face up to why I left this morning. Yes, Noah asked for my help with the horses because the trainer needed the morning off. But I was relieved to have an excuse to leave."

She sucked in a breath and glared at him. "I already know that. No need to be *this* honest, Axel."

"I want to be honest because you *do* mean a lot to me. I wasn't planning on falling for a guest this week, Sadie. I wasn't planning on being fake-engaged. I wasn't planning on sleeping with you.

But it all happened. And I was a jerk this morning for leaving. I wanted to say that most of all."

She stood, her pale brown eyes flashing. "If you say you're sorry I will push you in the creek, Axel Dawson."

He knew what she meant. She didn't want to hear sorry or regrets.

But he was sorry that he'd hurt her, that he was hurting her now.

"We have a few more days to get through," she said, arms crossed over her chest. "Let's get through them. I'll explain our lack of togetherness to my family by saying you're very busy. If you wouldn't mind showing up for my sister's wedding Saturday night in the lodge, I would appreciate it. We'll leave Sunday morning and that'll be that." Her voice was so tight, so clogged.

He stared at her, feeling something in his chest shift. "Of course I'm coming to the wedding."

"Great," she said. "We'll get through that and then this whole fake nonsense will be over."

"Sadie. There was nothing fake about last night. Nothing."

She lifted her chin and didn't say anything. "Well, I'd better get back. I miss Danny."

Me, too, he thought out of nowhere, but he did.

Chapter Thirteen

For the next two days, Sadie kept her and Danny booked with ranch activities so that she wouldn't have a spare moment to think about her aching chest and how much she missed the sight of Axel. She had seen him at a distance twice, and both times had hurt. She hadn't texted him and he hadn't texted her. When she wasn't learning how to ride a horse and taking Danny for butterfly-sighting walks along the creek and going to every educational talk about the animals in the petting zoo (she now knew that cows had four stomachs and that goats did not have front teeth on their upper jaws), she was helping Evie with her wedding checklists and making sure all was set for the big night.

Everyone wanted to know "where that handsome fiancé of yours is," including Danny, who kept asking for Zul.

"Mama, Zul tay?" her son asked as they left the cafeteria after lunch, Danny holding his superhero lion.

Toddler speak for *Will I see Axel today?* Sadie scooped Danny up in her arms. "Axel has been working super hard on the ranch but I think we'll see him today."

Danny's smile could turn any grump's frown upside down. He looked *so* happy.

Her heart clenched. On one hand, it wasn't fair to Danny to suddenly pull Axel from his life. On the other, that was how it would be once they were home. But they *weren't* home now, they were at the ranch and she should probably make the most of it for Danny and let him spend time with his hero. She put him on the ground and he flew his lion in the air, running in big circles.

"Zul! Zul!" Danny suddenly shouted and went sprinting toward the alpaca enclosure.

Sadie looked over. Oh, God, there he was. Looking incredibly sexy in dark jeans and the hunter green polo, a brown Stetson on his head.

Just like the first day we arrived, she thought,

*when Danny went running for the man who'd
saved him on Badger Mountain.*

Sadie slowly made her way closer, but not too
close. She watched as Axel scooped up Danny in
his arms and held him up high, giving him a big
smooch on the cheek. Danny wrapped his arms
around Axel's neck.

"Yoo-hoo! Sadie! Axel," Sadie's mom called,
heading over with Aunt Tabby, Vanessa and Izzy
in her wheelchair. Aunt Tabby and Viv had been
somewhere between small talk and real conversation the past couple of days, ever since Tabby
had opened up about having a date with Cowboy
Joe. Tonight, they'd be going on their third date
in three days.

Sadie stepped closer. If she acted like she and
Axel were having problems, which, of course, they
were, her mother would pester her for details.

"Listen, lovebirds, I have a great idea," Viv said.
"You two have barely seen each other the past two
days! Why don't you go into town and spend some
time together? There's a special scavenger hunt in
the kid zone and I'll bet Danny wants to find some
secret treasure."

Danny nodded vigorously and attempted to say
treasure. Viv plucked him right out of Axel's arms.

"Go ahead, we'll take care of our little precious," Viv said, kissing Danny on the head.

Sadie tried to think of a few reasons why she

couldn't go anywhere with Axel but nothing good was coming to her. She could barely think straight with those piercing blue eyes on her.

"I do need to go into town," Axel said, staring at Sadie. "We can run an errand and stop for an early dinner. Maybe that fish and chips place."

What was this? Was he kidding?

He looked dead serious. Oh, wait. He probably was planning to visit another address on the list from his dad and liked the idea of her coming along like the last two times. But Axel Dawson's personal life had nothing to do with her. Not anymore. They were still pretending to be engaged but they were not pretending to be friends.

"I, uh, thought I'd see if Evie needed any help with final wedding details," Sadie said. There— perfect excuse. The wedding was the day after tomorrow. Sadie had been gearing up for having Axel as her date, since that was a given, and talking herself through how on earth she'd deal with that.

"Actually, hon," Viv said, "Evie texted a little while ago. She's with her mother-in-law-to-be and grandmother-in-law-to-be today, picking up her dress and making sure the alterations are exact. Personally, I think *I* should have gone. I would have noticed if anything was even a smidge off!"

No one disagreed with that assessment of her skills.

"Oh," Sadie said.

Axel held out his arm. "Shall we go?"

Uh, he didn't have to go overboard, she thought, shooting him a surreptitious dagger.

She gave Danny a kiss goodbye, waved to her relatives and then off they walked, her hand around his arm. Once they were out of hearing distance, she pulled away. "And what was *that* about?"

"Just trying to keep up appearances, Sadie. Your mother is like a hawk. You heard her—she notices *smidges*."

Well, that was true. "I guess. But still. You didn't need to give me your arm. This isn't Regency England."

He raised an eyebrow. "I'm glad the suggestion was made to spend time together. I've missed you, Sadie. I was hoping we could talk."

"Is there anything to say? I'm looking for a husband and father for my son. One who's madly in love with Danny and with me. If that's not you, then…"

"Like I said the other day, Sadie, I didn't expect to fall for you."

She stopped in her tracks. Those words of his— from when they'd met at the rock at the creek—had swirled around her mind these past two days. She'd been such a walking ball of heartache that she'd almost missed it in the moment.

He'd fallen for her. He'd said it. And now he'd said it again.

She'd sat with it the past couple of days, wanting to give him time and space to maybe figure things out. If he'd fallen for her, he'd have to accept it. He might not have wanted to, but he had, and you couldn't stop a speeding train. And that was what love was. A locomotive.

But then no text, no call, no asking to see her. If Danny hadn't beelined for him just now, would he have asked to spend the afternoon with her in town? No, because he clearly hadn't accepted it.

"I've thought of little else but you and Danny these past two days. So many times I wanted to go see you but—"

She didn't want to do this. A repeat of the last conversation. She *couldn't* do this. But you know what? She was going to do something *else*. Work with what she had. She was in love with Axel Dawson. He was the man for her. He wasn't ready to see that, fine. But he'd given her what she needed to know: he hadn't meant to fall for her. But had.

"Do you have to go into town?" she asked.

He nodded. "I'd like to visit the next address on my dad's list. But I know I don't want to do it alone. And by alone, I mean specifically without you, Sadie. You're really good moral support."

He wanted to be with her. He needed her. And

he had fallen for her. She had the guy right where she wanted him, really. Right?

Because this was the same guy whose overheard conversation with his sister had ripped her heart in two.

Who said anything about love?

No one—which was why she was going to help get him there. The man loved her. She was pretty sure, anyway. Seventy-five percent sure. Axel had been hurt—and by a single mother with a baby—and was protecting himself, maybe without even realizing it. So hell yeah she was going to try.

"Well, when you put it that way," she said, taking his arm again. "Of course I'll go."

He looked into her eyes, and she could see relief cross his face. "Good. And thank you."

"Let's not talk about us, okay? Pinkie swear," she said, holding up her right one.

That would probably be more of a relief to him. And necessary to giving him some breathing room from any heaviosity. She'd just *be* today. And that would be enough.

He held up his left one. "Pinkie swear."

They wrapped pinkies.

A lovely breeze lifted her hair, and she raised her face to the gorgeous sunny weather. She was getting her mojo back where Axel was concerned. She felt more in control of her own destiny instead of allowing him to dictate and decide. She'd do what she could to make him see sense: that she was it for him. And if he didn't? As Mom and Aunt Tabby and Gram and Great-Gram would say: his flipping loss.

Of course, she'd be brokenhearted and sobbing for three days, but she'd know she'd tried, that she'd put herself out there for the future she wanted.

"So guess who the latest ranch romance is," Sadie said. "You will never believe this."

"Your aunt Tabby and Cowboy Joe?" he asked.

She gave him a gentle sock in the arm. "How did you know? It's brand-new. They've been on three dates in three days!"

"That's exactly how I do know. I saw them walking arm in arm by the creek, then feeding each other ice cream during off-hours in the caf yesterday, and a few hours ago, I saw them kissing goodbye behind your cabin."

Sadie grinned. "Whodathunk you could go to a family reunion and fall in love?" She almost choked the moment she realized what she'd said.

"I'm happy for them," he said. "Cowboy Joe is a great person. I've known him a long, long time." He pointed up ahead at his buggy, parked near the petting zoo. "There are the dancing alpacas. I mean, they're standing still but now when I look at them, I imagine them doing the Macarena."

She smiled and looked at them, the two furry

beasts standing so close to each other, their heads over the fence. Did he *have* to reference their night together? The wine that had helped lead to that killer kiss and everything else that had happened?

He must have caught the shift in her expression because he quickly added, "Sorry."

Channel Taylor Swift and shake it off, she told herself. "So," she began as they got into the buggy, "where are we headed?"

"An isolated ranch ten miles or so from here. The Hurley place. I don't know who they are or what connection my dad might have to them. Noah and Daisy didn't either."

They drove in silence, which she appreciated, enjoying the breeze through the half-open windows and the views of farmland. As they turned up the long drive for the Hurley ranch, Sadie could see up ahead that the house was not in great condition. The gray barn was peeling and there didn't seem to be any animals. Maybe it wasn't a working ranch.

As Axel pulled up to the house, a middle-aged man came out. He wore jeans and a cowboy hat.

"Who are you?" the man asked.

"My name is Axel Dawson and—"

A huge grin broke out on the man's face. "Dawson? Why didn't you start with that?" He held out his hand. "You one of Bo's kids? I know he had a lot of 'em."

"Smack in the middle of six." He turned to Sadie. "This is Sadie Winston."

The man nodded at her. "I was real sorry to hear he passed. We were away and missed the funeral. We owe everything to Bo Dawson," he said, gesturing with his chin toward the house. "I'm Matt Hurley. I live here with my wife, Sue. Our two kids are grown and off on their own, thanks to Bo."

Axel did a double take at that. "Thanks to Bo?"

"Up until about a year ago, I used to drink heavily. Bo helped me out a time or two, brought me home, got me in bed. My wife threatened to leave me. Bo got me to quit, gave me a lot of pamphlets to read, took me to meetings. I cleaned up my act because of him."

"Wait. My father? He was drunk himself eighty percent of the time."

"He got worse toward the end, I guess," Matt said. "No one knew he was dying. He kept that a secret. I think he drank more then. But he'd said his kids were mad at him and wanted him to stop and so he tried and said we'd do it together. And he got me to stop. I thought he stopped, too. He said nothing was more important than family. Certainly not a bottle of Jack Daniel's or cheap beer."

Sadie squeezed Axel's hand. Every time she learned more about his dad, she heard something that made him sound like the hero he must have taught Axel to be. Not perfect. Far from it. He'd done his share of damage. But he'd done good, too.

Matt took off his hat and held it to his chest, as if in honor of Bo. "If it weren't for Bo Dawson, my two boys wouldn't be speaking to me right now. My wife would be married to someone else. Your dad saved my hide."

Axel put his hand on the man's shoulder. "Thanks for telling me. It's nice to know."

"Why'd you come by, anyway?" Matt asked.

Axel showed him the list of addresses. "My dad left this for me. No annotations, nothing. Just the addresses. He must have wanted me to know about you and maybe to check in."

"Stop by anytime and bring your girlfriend," Matt said, smiling at her. "Any kid of Bo Dawson is family to me and Sue."

We're actually engaged, Sadie almost said.

Matt hugged them both and headed back inside. For a few moments, she and Axel just stood and looked at the house, at the barn, and Sadie could imagine he was thinking of his dad walking up those steps, helping someone out, doing for Matt what he wouldn't let anyone do for him.

Finally, Axel took her hand as they walked to the SUV. She could hold his hand forever.

"He wanted me to know he was a good person, in case I'd forgotten," Axel said, opening the pas-

senger door for her. "That's what the list of addresses is about."

Sadie nodded. "Looks that way."

"The more I learn about him, the more I don't
think I knew my dad at all," he said. "And I thought
I did. I thought I had him all figured out."

"People are that way. Even the ones closest to
us."

He buckled up and then looked at her. "There's
one more address but I've been shocked enough
for one day. Why don't we drive into town and go
get coffee and walk around?"

"Perfect day for it."

So they did. They got iced coffees from Java
Jamboree and walked along Main Street, stopping
at the dog park to watch the little dogs yip and
sniff each other.

"Suit for Evie's wedding or a tux?" he asked as
a tan pug stared at them.

"No doggy treats, sorry," she told the cute little
pug, and they resumed walking. "Evie said anything goes for the dress code. No one came here
expecting to attend a wedding on the final night,
and no one came to a dude ranch with a fancy out-
fit. Though none of us live all that far away, she
doesn't want anyone having to drive home and
back. It's come as you are."

"I'll wear a suit since I don't have that excuse.
My fancy clothes *are* at the dude ranch."

She could see him all dressed up. At least her final night at the Dawson Family Guest Ranch would be amazing. Her dear sister married. Axel beside her in his suit. The next morning she and Danny would go home, back to real life, and this would all seem a dream. The fake engagement and the one incredible night she'd shared with Axel.

Maybe it was all just a fantasy she had to let go of instead of trying to make Axel see his sister was right—that when you found love like this you grabbed it and never let it go.

Who said anything about love?

Was she flattering herself that he felt about her the way she did about him? She knew he adored Danny. And the way he'd been with her on his couch, in his bed—that hadn't been just sex.

I'm saying something about love, she thought as he stopped in front of Bear Ridge Ice Cream and Candy, so good that she often drove out of her way to come out here.

"I could go for a double scoop of mint chocolate chip and maybe coffee chip or chocolate peanut butter," he said. "In a waffle cone."

"Don't tell Danny we stopped here. He loves this place."

"I wish he were here," he said. "I've missed him terribly the past couple of days."

"He's gotten to you, huh?" she asked even

though she was the one who'd said they shouldn't talk about them. Danny counted as them.

Please say, Yes, I love that kid like he's my own flesh and blood, and in fact, I love you, too.

"He got to me on Badger Mountain. Just like you did."

"And this week?" she asked, practically holding her breath.

"This week has been scary as hell," he said. "I'm engaged, about to become a dad." He smiled.

Oh. He was kidding about the scary as hell. When he'd said that, she thought, *Yup, this man loves me like* crazy. Now she wasn't so sure.

He held her gaze for a moment, everything he was flashing in his blue eyes. She wanted to kiss him, wrap her arms around him, hold him tight and never let him go.

But a group of teens were trying to exit the busy shop and the moment was gone in a snap, ice cream choices their biggest concern.

Ice cream was a lot easier than figuring out how he felt. She knew that was true as she studied the sign announcing the flavors and looked at the big containers in the display case.

"I'm thinking double fudge brownie," she said, eyeing the delicious-looking ice cream. "You set on what you're getting?"

Silence.

She glanced up and Axel was standing ramrod straight, the color blanched from his face.

"Hello," a woman said stiffly, looking at Axel, then at Sadie, then at the door. The woman was in her early thirties, tall and slender, with shoulder-length auburn hair. She held a dish of ice cream in her hand; the cute little girl at her side, maybe three or four years old, licked a scoop on a cone. The woman took the girl's free hand and hurried her out.

Axel still didn't move.

Sadie glanced out the window; the woman and girl were gone. *Oh*, she thought. *Ohhh. I certainly know who they were.* The ex who'd left him and her daughter, whom he'd been so attached to and never seen again.

Till now.

"You okay?" she asked. "We can skip the ice cream if you just saw a ghost."

He glanced at her. "How'd you know?"

"Because I know *you*."

"I'm fine," he said and glanced up at the teenager behind the counter. "Sadie, what'll it be?"

His forced smile didn't fool her. He wasn't fine. One of the biggest reasons that kept him insisting marriage and a family weren't for him had just walked out of the shop.

Either running into the woman and her daughter would give him some kind of necessary closure that he'd been lacking or he'd brood on it and it would make him retreat further behind that brick wall he'd built around himself.

Which was it?

Please be the former, she thought, suddenly having no appetite for ice cream.

Chapter Fourteen

"Well, I think we should *all* go," Aunt Tabby said, staring at Viv.

"I think *you* should go if you want to," Viv snapped. "Count me out."

The guest cabin wasn't big enough for all these women and their arguments. Aunt Tabby stood in the arched doorway to the living room, glaring at her sister on the window seat. Sadie and Evie were on the sofa, and Vanessa was knitting socks—Sadie was pretty sure they were for Axel, unfortunately—on the rocker near where Danny sat piling his beloved blocks.

Viv and Tabby had been arguing all morning about whether or not the group should go on the wilderness tour up Clover Mountain, an easy mile loop without steep inclines. Izzy would be going on the bird-watching adventure along the creek with another group of relatives since a hike would be too much for her. Today was the last day for a guided hike since tomorrow was Evie's wedding and they'd spend the day preparing for the big event after sunrise yoga.

Sadie certainly wouldn't mind the forced proximity to her fake fiancé, who'd be leading the tour. He'd made himself scarce since they'd returned from Bear Ridge yesterday. On the drive home, he hadn't mentioned the ex and her little girl, and Sadie hadn't either, though she was full of questions. Did you want to marry her? Had you proposed? Had the ex been The One and no one else could compare?

Those kinds of awful questions had kept her up last night. She hadn't heard from Axel since or seen him around the ranch.

"This is our family reunion," Tabby pointed out, her voice nearly breaking. "We should all go on the *family* hike!"

Sadie looked at Evie, who was sitting on the other end of the couch, going over the seating arrangements. Sadie could tell her sister was trying to ignore the bickering.

"Been there, not doing that again," Viv said, crossing her arms over her chest. "End of story." She glanced at Evie. "Honey, remember not to put Grandpa next to Uncle Robby. They always argue about politics. Separate tables."

"Oh, right," Evie said. "If only I could concentrate while my mother and aunt are arguing loudly." She shot each woman a pointed look.

"Your mother is the queen of obstinate!" Tabby said.

"Says the princess without a country!" Viv countered.

"How dare you," Tabby snapped.

"Mom, Tabby, please," Sadie said. "Danny can hear you."

At the sound of his name, Danny glanced up from where he was piling a tower of blocks.

Both women looked chastised but tossed each other a final scowl.

"Besides," Evie said, turning off her iPad and stretching, "as the bride, I decide everything the twenty-four hours before my wedding, right? It's a new Bridezilla tradition. And I say we *all* go on the hike."

"But—" Viv began.

"Mom, listen," Sadie said. "Maybe all of us going on another hike with Danny, seeing him safe, not getting lost, will help you and Aunt Tabby put the past behind you. Until you deal with it, since you won't *talk* about it, you'll never get past it."

Evie nodded. "Exactly. And you have to both go. It's what I want as a wedding gift. I mean that."

Viv eyed her younger daughter. "Oh, fine."

"Fine," Tabby snapped.

It did sound fine to Sadie. She had a feeling Evie was right and that their mom and aunt would work out their issues on Family Hike 2.0.

She also had to admit she liked the idea of knowing she'd see Axel later. Even for an hour and shared with many of her relatives.

This morning, Axel was riding parallel to the pasture trails to make sure not a single Winston fell off their horse. Now that the family reunion was winding down, many in the group wanted to try activities they hadn't earlier in the week. Horseback riding was one.

He was glad to be on horseback himself, his mind on patrol and safety. Last night, seeing his ex and her daughter, now a little girl instead of the baby he knew, had played over and over in his mind like a recording. Lizzie's stiff hello, the girl, whose name was Jolie, enjoying her cone, the hurry out the door. He was grateful for that last one.

Interesting thing was, Axel hadn't felt anything for his ex. He always thought if he ran into her, he'd be brought to his knees, but he'd felt nothing, except for the shock of actually seeing her. Even her daughter hadn't really registered, most likely because she looked nothing like the baby she'd been. There was no connection.

What he did feel was a strange sense of rein-forcement, the reshoring up of his complete lack of interest in going through that again.

Sadie wanted him to set himself up for the pos-sibility.

He couldn't. He'd taken the advice of the moun-tain man who'd told him to be the boss of his emo-tions and run with it, so far and wide that Axel himself wasn't the boss. Or that was how it felt, anyway. He knew he had serious feelings for Sadie and her son. But something even more powerful was keeping him back.

He could hear Daisy yell up a storm if she got wind of that. *And you're gonna let whatever that is win?* she'd demand.

He turned Goldie around and stayed in line a good hundred yards from three teens on quarter horses, keeping an eagle eye on them. They were talking and laughing and having a good time, but not so focused on the land or their horses. They weren't far from the stables, but Axel would keep his mind on his job and not on Sadie. Hard as it was.

He was leading a wilderness tour later today and he wondered if she'd show up. He wanted to see her so bad he couldn't stop picturing her beautiful face. Then Danny's sweet face and mop of blond hair, Zul waving around high over his head, would pop into his mind.

Axel thought about what Sadie had overheard: *Who said anything about love?* The pain it had caused her, the change between them.

When he thought about the word love and Sadie and Danny Winston, something in him shuttered. Closed up, closed off.

For a guy who was in charge of safety, should he be this damned scared?

Axel sure knew his wild berries and trees and leaves and worms and caterpillars, Sadie thought as the group walked up Clover Mountain, which was just a flat wooded trail with ever-so-slight inclines now and again. He had the entire group hanging on his every word as he pointed out which berries were edible and which would give you the stomachache from hell. They'd been hiking for about forty minutes and would turn around at the hour mark, taking a break for water and cereal bars. Danny sure would sleep well tonight. He'd done a lot of walking. Right now, they were in a clearing surrounded by dense woods, and there were so many birds and butterflies that Danny was constantly entertained.

A western meadowlark with its yellow belly

flew to a low branch were Danny was standing, and Danny shouted, "Yell bird" and went racing after it.

"Danny!" Sadie called after him. "Always wait for the group!"

Danny kept going, but this time, Axel was near and scooped him up.

"Gotcha!" he said. "Wilderness hiking means staying with your group, right, buddy?"

Axel had given a three-minute prehike talk about exactly that and hike safety before they'd started walking. He managed to look incredibly sexy in his staff shirt and khaki cargo shorts. And with Danny in his arm, he looked like a dad.

She wished Axel could see himself the way she saw him.

"But yell bird," Danny said.

"You can see the yellow bird if you look up in the trees. See, there's one!" Axel said, pointing.

Danny flew his superhero lion around in circles where Axel was pointing.

"This is exactly what happened last time," Viv said, hands on hips as she glared at her sister. "I asked you to keep an eye on Danny not thirty seconds ago so I could have my cereal bar early. And what happens? He goes racing off to who knows where!"

Sadie froze. What was going on here? Danny was fine. And this hike was supposed to make things better between her mother and aunt—not worse.

Tabby's eyes misted. "He didn't run off this time. He was right ahead of us and Axel was there."

"He could have run in any direction," Viv said. "Luckily, Axel was up ahead and paying attention."

Tabby burst into tears and dropped on an uncomfortable-looking rock. "I feel awful about what happened on Badger Mountain. I've apologized a million times for not paying closer attention. I can't possibly feel worse, Viv."

Viv's expression remained stony. She crossed her arms over her chest.

"Mom, seriously?" Sadie said.

Evie was shaking her head.

"Danny was lost for two hours!" Viv said. "Just like—" She clamped her mouth shut and turned away. "Just forget it," she added, throwing her hands up in the air.

Evie stepped closer to Viv. "Just like who?"

"Just like Tabby, that's who. When we were kids, she ran off when I was supposed to be watching her. She was missing until close to midnight."

Vanessa gasped. "Oh, Vivvy. You can't possibly blame yourself for that. You were a kid. You were only nine! Tabby was five."

"Wait a minute," Sadie said. "Why don't I know this story?"

"Or me," Evie asked.

"My mother said that Tabby and I could pick flowers," Viv explained. "But there was a butterfly and Tabby chased it and I got tired of running after her so I kept picking flowers. But she never came back." Their grandparents' house abutted woodlands. Sadie and Evie used to love playing in there as kids, annoyed that their mother always insisted on coming with them, keeping them in sight. Now Sadie knew why.

Tabby looked incredulous that Viv remembered this. "Well, I did. Because I'm right here fifty years later."

"It was my fault," Viv said. "I didn't pay attention to where you were, that you weren't close by anymore. It was the most sickening feeling not to know where you were."

"Viv, I don't remember that," Tabby said. "I mean, I remember it coming up a few times, Mom and Dad reminding me to stay close. But I don't remember being lost."

"I do," Viv said, her brown eyes teary. "Mom does."

Vanessa put a hand on Viv's shoulder. "I remember being scared, like any mother would be. Like Sadie was when Danny was lost. But I certainly didn't blame you, honey. I wouldn't have blamed you if it had happened when you were ten or twenty or now. People run off when you're not looking sometimes. Danny getting lost wasn't Tabby's fault. Just like it wasn't your fault when she got lost."

"I guess the whole thing brought all that up in me," Viv said. "Such an old event. But so close to the surface, I guess. That fear, I can still remember it so vividly."

Evie nodded. "So Danny going missing reminded you of it and maybe these past three months, you've really been mad at yourself."

"Sounds like you've never forgiven yourself, Viv," Axel said.

Viv glanced at all of them, then turned to her sister. "I'm sorry, Tabby. I've been awful the past few months."

"You sure have been," Tabby said with a smile. She opened her arms and Viv embraced her, the two sisters hugging tight.

"Oh, you," Viv said, wiping under her eyes.

Sadie smiled. "Well, turns out this hike *was* a good idea."

"Snack?" Danny said and it was the perfect icebreaker to a lighter mood. Everyone laughed and there were hugs all around.

"How about we have our snack right here on this special location forever known as Sister Make Up Point, and then we'll turn back," Axel said.

"Ooh, our own point!" Viv said, her eyes lighting up. "Will that be added to the guidebooks?"

She was serious. Sadie sent Axel a smile.

Axel grinned. "It might be unofficial but important nonetheless."

"Snack?" Danny asked again.

Gram and Gray-Aunt Tabby had his strawberry cereal bar and water bottle, so he ran to them, and they sat on rocks and chatted about the walk. The sight of the three of them, the feud over and done, lifted a big weight off Sadie's chest.

A phone buzzed, and Sadie glanced around. It was Evie's. Her sister smiled at the phone in her hand and walked a few feet away to answer. That smile meant it was Marshall—or Marshy as she liked to call him.

"Oh no, you didn't!" Evie yelped into her phone. Her expression was pure fury.

Uh, what?

"No, you are not inviting your ex-girlfriend to the wedding," Evie said, "and that's final! Do you see me inviting my exes to the wedding? No. Because it's not done." She listened. "Oh, really? Well, I guess the wedding is off, then!" She shoved her phone in her pocket and burst into tears.

Oh no. What the heck was this? Marshall Ackerman, usually supernice and thoughtful, wanted his ex at his wedding? Had he gone *insane*?

Sadie glanced at her mom, aunt and grand-mother; they looked as worried as Sadie felt.

"Evie, I'm sure that with a few minutes to think about it, he'll uninvite her," their mom assured her. "If it's that important to you, that's what matters."

"He says if it's that important to him, it should be important to me!" Evie said. "Just because they were together from middle school through college and she was a big part of his life doesn't mean she gets to be at my wedding."

"Is she married?" Sadie asked.

Evie shook her head. "No! She has a serious boyfriend, apparently, but still. She probably still loves Marshall. She's the old part of his life. I'm the present and future!"

"Evie, just call him and tell him you'd feel un-comfortable," Aunt Tabby said. "I get it. And I rarely take your side when you and Marshall are arguing."

That was true. Tabby didn't play devil's advo-cate so much as be willing to tell Evie when she was overreacting or being too self-centered.

Evie's phone buzzed. She looked at the screen and seemed to be reading texts. "Oh, really!" she bellowed at it. "Well, I guess we're not getting married!" She shoved her phone in her pocket again and stalked off beside a tree.

"Aunt Evie mad," Danny said.

Sadie ruffled Danny's thick blond hair. "Aunt

Evie got into an argument with someone. That means they both want their way about the same thing. But they'll work it out. Family always does."

Danny got bored fast. "Zul?" he held out his arms, and Axel picked him up.

Axel smiled at Danny, then turned to Sadie. "I've got him. You deal with this."

Sadie nodded and went to Evie. "Evie, meet him in person and talk this out. You're getting married tomorrow night!"

"Guess not!" Evie said, sparks shooting from her brown eyes. She was spitting mad.

"Now you listen to me, Evie Winston," Sadie barked. "You are engaged for real, unlike me, when getting married to the man I love is all I want. There is no way you're calling off your—"

Sadie froze, her mistake ringing in her ears. Oh no. Oh, dear.

Please tell me I didn't say that out loud.

Even Evie, in her tizzy, caught the slip. "Unlike you?"

"Yeah," Viv said. "What do you mean, unlike you?"

Everyone was staring at Sadie.

Sadie glanced at Axel, who gave her a sympathetic look.

"Engaged for real, *unlike me*?" Tabby repeated. "So you're not engaged?"

"I don't understand this at all," Vanessa said. "Are Sadie and Axel engaged?"

"Let Sadie explain herself," Viv said. "Pipe down, everyone."

Oh foo. She sucked in a breath. "Axel and I are not engaged. We never were."

"What?" Viv bellowed.

All eyes were on Sadie. She wanted to run down the mountain and hide but she had to get this over with. Maybe it was for the best that the truth had come out. Telling everyone when they got home to Prairie City that Axel had broken their engagement and it was over? A lie too many. That wasn't who Sadie Winston was.

"The night Evie got engaged," she began, "Axel walked me back to the cabin. I told Gram the news about Evie and Marshall, and she said something like 'They're engaged!' and ran in to make her phone calls, and that's when Izzy came out to see what the hoopla was about and mistook me and Axel for the engaged couple. Izzy was so happy for me she cried. She said she could go gentle into that good night knowing her divorced great-granddaughter who'd been through so much heartache had found love with a true hero."

"I guess I can see Izzy saying that," Viv said, arms crossed on her chest, of course.

"I can vouch for it. I was there," Axel put in. He still held Danny, who was not paying a lick of attention to the boring grown-up conversation. He was talking to Zul the lion in a low voice, telling him about his new powers.

A bunch of eyes turned to Axel with glares. He'd gone from can-do-no-wrong Axel to big, fat liar.

"So neither of us corrected Izzy," Sadie continued. "And then she went to sleep. I figured I'd tell Gram what happened, but Gram was on the phone sharing the big news about Evie and Marshall for hours. I didn't get the chance. By the time I woke up, Izzy had spread the word that Axel and I were engaged, and everyone thought both Evie and I had gotten engaged that night."

"You could have said this that morning!" Viv's eyes narrowed.

"I know, Mom, but then you and Tabby were talking for the first time in months because you thought both Winston girls were engaged. And you, Evie, you told me you hadn't wanted to get engaged while I, a single mother, was alone. You said my getting engaged meant everything to you. How could I tell you—"

"Oh, God," Evie said. "I remember that conversation in the cabin. I can understand why you didn't pipe up."

"So it was all a misunderstanding?" Vanessa asked. "You're *not* engaged?"

Sadie shook her head. "No. I'm not."

"And you went along with this?" Viv asked Axel. He nodded. "I did. And I'd do it again."

"Trust me that being fake-engaged to me wasn't easy for him," Sadie said, trying not to look at him.

"Well, that was kind of you for Sadie's sake," Viv said. "But I'm still mad at both of you. I guess I understand how it happened, though."

Evie nodded. "I totally understand how it happened. I'm sorry, Sadie."

Aw. That meant Evie got it, understood all the muckety-muck that led to her keeping up the ruse.

Sadie hugged Evie, whose eyes were misty.

"I guess I can also see how you felt like you had to keep it up," Viv said. "We do have a habit of dominating conversations and not letting anyone get a word in."

"By *we*, she means me, too," Tabby said. "And Gram."

"Guilty," Vanessa said, holding up her hand. "Sorry, honey. I hope we didn't make you feel like getting engaged is the be-all and end-all. You know that's not how I feel."

"I know," Sadie said. "I got caught up in the hoopla myself. To be honest, I liked being engaged. Even pretend."

Everyone's eyes turned to Axel, who was still holding Danny, waving his superhero lion flying above his head. Viv took out her camera and snapped a photo of the two of them. Axel looked like a deer caught in headlights.

Her mother stared at her for a moment as if she was putting more than two and two together. Sadie had no idea what Viv was thinking.

"Just in case we don't see you after tonight, Axel," Viv said. "I'll text you the photo to remember Danny by."

Sadie swallowed. Viv wanted Axel to have a photo of what he could have because her mother knew that her daughter was madly in love with the guy.

And the look on Axel's face told a different story. A story with an ending that said, *I'm free. I'm finally free.* She felt tears sting her eyes, and she blinked them away.

"I don't think we should tell Izzy till we get home," Vanessa said. "It'll be too confusing. Let's just enjoy Evie's wedding. There *will* be a wedding, right?"

Now all eyes swung to Evie.

"As long as the ex-girlfriend isn't coming, yes," she said. "Marshy will put me first, right? I mean, my feelings have to be more important on this than having his old girlfriend at his wedding."

"Evie, honey," Tabby said. "Why don't you call Marshall and tell him the wedding is definitely on, but his girlfriend ain't coming and that's that."

Evie called. They all waited. "Marshall, the

wedding is on, but your ex is not coming and that's that." She listened, and Sadie's entire body felt like it was on pins and needles.

"I know. No, I know. I know."

What did she know?

"She knows what?" Tabby whispered.

Viv shrugged.

"No, *you're* the best," Evie said. "No, *I'm* sorry. I love you, too. Bye, sweetie." Evie pocketed her phone, now beaming. Phew.

Sadie smiled. Now that was a good ending to a story.

"The wedding is on," Evie said.

There were cheers and claps.

"I'll take my grandson," Viv said, plucking Danny from Axel. "You and Sadie probably have some loose ends to tie up. I hope you're still going to be her date at the wedding. I mean, we did order you a filet mignon and made up the seating arrangements, so it would spoil everything if you bailed on us."

Oh, Mom. I do love you.

"Of course I'll be there," Axel said. "I mean, if Sadie wants me to be."

Evie squeezed Sadie's hand. "C'mon," she said, gesturing for the relatives to start down the trail. "Let's let them talk."

Sadie waited until the group was far enough

ahead not to hear. "I guess you're officially off the hook."

"I would like to attend the wedding, by the way. And not just because my dinner was ordered and I'd mess up the seating arrangements."

"You actually want to spend more time with my family than you have to?" she asked.

"Your family is fantastic, Sadie. They're wonderful. You really are lucky."

"I know. Sometimes they're smothering. But always in a good way."

He smiled. "The wedding will be a really nice ending to a special week."

Really nice. Ending. Special week.

It was over. He was going to say goodbye. After everything they'd been through? Shared together?

Her heart broke. It had been breaking ever since the morning she'd woken up alone in his bed, when she knew she'd gotten herself in over her head, but now it cracked completely in two.

"Evie hired a great band," she said, trying not to cry.

"See you tomorrow night, then."

"See you," she said.

And then they started down the mountain. Together but very much separate.

Chapter Fifteen

In the morning, the entire cabin went to sunrise yoga, including Izzy, who did some moves from her wheelchair. Then they went to the caf for breakfast, where Cowboy Joe had a crepe station in honor of the bride, who lived for crepes of all kinds. The handsome cook would be Tabby's date for Evie's wedding that night.

"Crazy, huh?" her mother whispered as Sadie gave Danny's mouth a dab with a napkin—strawberry and cream crepes were delicious but messy. "We come here to honor Axel, and two of the closest people to

us find love. Evie and Marshall not only got back together, but engaged. And Tabby is in love."

"Thank you for not mentioning my fake love,"
Sadie whispered back.

"You okay?" Viv asked.

"I'll be okay. I have to be. Danny comes first."

"You fell for him, huh?" Viv asked. "Hard."

Sadie nodded. "Head over heels. But he told me
not to on day one. I just didn't listen."

"You listened, hon. You just went with your
heart. To me, that's the best way. It means you
tried, you risked, you put yourself out there."

Unlike Axel.

"Axel's flipping loss," her mom added, shaking her head.

Sadie smiled. She called that one. "So you and
Tabby are good now?"

"I feel terrible for how I acted. Blaming her for
my precious grandson going missing when it wasn't
her fault he ran off in a split second. All because
the whole thing triggered a childhood memory—
a scary one for me. I didn't even know that epi-
sode was still bothering me, but it sure was. All
these years."

"I can understand, Mom. You were scared for
your little sister."

Plus, she better understood now that some scars
ran deep.

Viv leaned close and kissed Sadie's cheek. "I

think Axel will come around. The way he looks at you, Sadie. And it's so clear he loves Danny."

"I don't know. I think I have to face facts. Enough pretending, right? The truth is the truth."

"Well, if you do have to let go of him, I can fix you up with my dentist's nephew. He's quite a catch."

Sadie smiled. "Thank you, Mom."

Viv gave her a one-armed shoulder squeeze and went back to her honey-banana crepe. Sadie poked hers around on her plate. She couldn't imagine ever being ready for more blind dates. How could any guy ever measure up to Axel Dawson?

Cowboy Joe came over with his big smile and trademark brown Stetson to deliver a box of chocolate rugelach to Tabby. "Enough to share with the whole cabin," he said. That got him a kiss from his girlfriend, who was beaming.

Sadie might be leaving her heart here when she left, but she loved that her aunt was so happy. She glanced at Evie, who was assuring Izzy that there was plenty of Frank Sinatra and Etta James in the song rotation. Marshall had come over last night, full of apology about suggesting his old girlfriend attend the wedding. Apparently, the two had run into each other in town earlier that day, and Marshall was so excited about marrying the woman of his dreams that he'd invited the ex—no more to it than that. Evie had felt much better about the whole thing.

Little things, big things—you never knew what would get you and whip you up, Sadie thought. She didn't want to let Axel go, but maybe she had to. He had his little things and big things and right now, they were stronger than his feelings for her. Ugh, she hated even thinking that, but it was true, right?

At the back of the cafeteria, she noticed Axel's sister, Daisy, and sister-in-law, Sara, restocking the grab-and-go bars on either side of the doors. The two women were chatting and, if Sadie wasn't imagining things, looking in her direction. She had a feeling they were discussing the Winston guest Axel had gotten fake-engaged to. Before she left tomorrow morning, Sadie would take Daisy aside and thank her for trying to push her brother when it came to matters of the heart, matters of *his* heart.

But at least she had tonight with him, and there was nothing fake about it. He'd be her date fair and square. She'd have a night to remember, and then she'd try, hard as she could, to move on.

Axel was on his second mug of coffee when his doorbell rang. Good chills ran up his spine at the idea that it was Sadie, whom he hadn't seen since they'd come down Clover Mountain. Even if she was here to tell him off, that he was no hero after all if he was afraid of the three of them—him, her and Danny—he'd be glad to see her face.

And he already knew he wasn't a hero.

That wilderness tour had been unexpectedly eventful but not in the terrible way that would send a search and rescue specialist into overdrive. Sadie's mother and aunt had finally made up. And his and Sadie's phony engagement had come to a sudden stop.

If it were Daisy at the door, asking him if he missed being fake-engaged even just a bit, he'd say no, of course not. But the truth was, he did miss it. He'd liked being paired with Sadie. He'd liked the hugs and warm wishes, and that had surprised him almost more than anything. Being part of something so…special even when it wasn't real had given him something of a spring in his step, as his gramps used to say.

And now he was back to being on his own, just Axel, the way he supposedly liked it. He'd take a day or two to shake off all that had happened, to get used to Sadie and her thirty-eight relatives being gone from the ranch, from his daily world, and his life would go on.

He went to the door and did a double take. "I am not seeing my brother Rex standing on my porch. This has to be a mirage." The sun *was* bright, not a cloud in the sky, but Rex Dawson, the middle of the Zeke, Rex, Axel trio, definitely was standing there. All the Dawson siblings resembled each other. Rex was tall and muscular with dark hair and blue eyes. He wasn't in his usual dark suit and Stetson, which meant he wasn't on the way to the airport or a meeting and had some time to spend. No one in the family knew exactly what Rex did for a living. FBI? Spy? Something secretive.

Rex grinned. "Oh, it's me all right. In the area on business and thought I'd come by and see everyone. First stop had to be your cabin. Daisy had told me it was luxe woodsman, and she didn't do it justice. *I* could live here." Rex lived in hotels since he did so much traveling, but at heart he was a cowboy, just like all the Dawson siblings.

"See, everyone says that when they see it. It tends to remind them of a lodge at a fancy ski resort or dude ranch."

Rex looked around. "Well, the lodge here is nice, but this is spectacular. Kudos to you. I thought you'd never come back here, Axel, but I can see how you can live here."

He hadn't told Rex or Zeke about the contents of the letter Bo had left him or learning about how their mom had met their dad. He had a lot to fill Rex in on.

In minutes, Axel and Rex were on the sofa in the living room, Dude at Axel's feet and coffee and Cowboy Joe's famed doughnuts in front of them. Axel told him the whole story, everything, and didn't bother leaving anything out. He and Rex didn't see each other often, but he'd always felt close to the guy. Same with Zeke and Ford. Axel had gotten almost *too* close with Noah and Daisy the past months. But he wouldn't trade the ability to talk to them about anything *for* anything.

"Sounds like this woman got to you," Rex said, popping a piece of cinnamon-sugar doughnut in his mouth.

"She did. But she wants the whole thing—marriage, a big family."

"And what do you want?" Rex asked. "Really?"

"To see them often." And that was true. He wanted to see them every day.

Zeke laughed. "So you want a relationship with Sadie, just on your terms."

"Yes," Axel said, grimacing. "I hear how it sounds, but yes. Why pretend I can deal with more than that?"

"You pretended exactly that for a week and seemed to like it just fine," Rex pointed out.

"Something's holding me back. I'm not totally sure what it even is. But it's stronger than I am, and you know what I can bench."

"Knocked out by your own punch," Rex said, sipping his coffee. "Now that's dumb."

He supposed it was, if his brother *had* to put it that way.

"Can you stay awhile?" Axel asked. "You're welcome to the guest room."

Rex shook his head. "I'm leaving late this afternoon. Another meeting in Jackson tomorrow."

"Ever gonna tell us exactly what it is you do?"

"One of these days," Rex said.

Axel hoped so, out of pure curiosity. "You ever get tired of all those meetings, all that travel, all those suits? I mean that in both senses."

Rex laughed. "Yes. Trust me." They finished off the doughnuts and had another round of coffee. "So. About Dad's letter. Maybe I could come along on the last address."

Axel raised an eyebrow. Rex had always been quiet about his take on Bo Dawson, keeping his feelings to himself. That he wanted to experience whatever good would come out of that final address was saying something. "You ever gonna tell us what was in the letter Dad left you?"

"I don't really want to talk about my letter," Rex said—and then looked immediately uncomfortable, like his shirt was suddenly squeezing the life out of him.

"I get it. It took me almost nine months to even open mine."

Rex sipped his coffee. "I'm curious what the last address is."

"Me, too. The first three helped—a lot."

"Not enough, though, Ax. Not if this Sadie is about to be the one who got away."

"I thought I was the one who got away."

Rex smiled and shook his head. "Nope. And you'll probably find that out in a week or two."

"Too much chitchat," Axel said, feeling like *his* shirt was getting too tight. "Let's go see what this last address is."

His phone pinged with a text. Daisy.

Hey, can you watch Tony for about an hour from one to two-ish? I want to check over the lodge and make sure everything is set up for the wedding.

You can get two brother babysitters for the price of one, he texted back. Rex is here.

Yay! she texted in reply.

"Looks like a little babysitting, then we'll hit the road," Axel told Rex.

"Good thing the back seat of my Jeep is full of presents for people under a year old," he said. "I might have bought out Baby Town before I drove over."

Axel smiled. Rex had better watch out or he'd be next on Daisy's hit list to get him married and adding a baby cousin to their brood.

Ahhh, if you had to have a broken heart, it helped to be sitting in a massage chair with heat functions at Esme's Day Spa in Prairie City, getting a pedicure. The bridal party would all have the same shade on their toes: Rouge Decadence, which was a sparkly bright red that Sadie loved. They'd already gotten their nails done in Ballet Slipper, a very pale pink, and had rejuvenating facials with potions and creams and cucumber slices over their eyes—that had been heavenly. Next, they'd be off to hair—beachy waves for everyone. Evie might be a serious CPA, but she was a skilled makeup artist who always did the family's faces for events—including her own wedding. Sadie wouldn't mind if this day went on forever.

"So I have an evil idea," Evie whispered. "Involving your date for tonight."

"Uh-oh," Sadie said while the pedicurist slathered a deliciously scented scrub on her legs.

"It's a risk, but might be worth it. And hey, I took a risk by giving Marshall an ultimatum, but it knocked some sense into him. So I say risk is good."

Sadie eyed her sister, intrigued and scared at the same time. "Exactly what did you have in mind?"

"I'm thinking you go see Axel in person. Not a text, not a call. Face-to-face. You tell him you appreciate all he's done for you this week, and that's why you're truly letting him off the hook by accepting another date for the wedding."

"But he already said he wants to go," Sadie pointed out.

"Yes, yes, he did. And do you want to know *why* he wants to go? Because he's in love with you and wants to be with you but isn't there yet. He needs a little push."

"I don't know, Evie. I've played enough games."

"This isn't a game," she said seriously. "Your happiness is important to me, Sadie. I don't care about deposits and plate costs. I care about you. And why the hell should Axel get to sit next to you and be your date at this special event when he's not planning to be your date ever again?"

Well, when she put it that way. Ouch.

"What I mean is," Evie continued, "maybe Axel should know that you're starting fresh—with another date to the wedding. Unless you *really* want him as your date, Evie. I know you're in love with the guy. But isn't tonight going to hurt?"

"It will either way," Sadie said, her stomach twisting.

"Yeah. I know. That's why I think you should give my evil plan a try. It might be the push that Axel Dawson needs."

Maybe? "I'll think about it while I'm getting my hair fussed over," Sadie said.

But she already knew her sister was on to something. Having Axel as her date to such an important event in her life *would* hurt. All night she'd just be wishing it meant something more than...friendship or a final favor of sorts. She'd slow dance with him and— Oh, who was she kidding? She'd never get through one dance in his arms without crying. She'd never be able to listen to Frank Sinatra again.

"Marshall has several interesting, attractive friends who would love to be moved from the singles table to be your plus-one," Evie said. "Just let me know."

"To be honest, Evie, I'd rather have no date than a stand-in. If I uninvited Axel, I mean."

"I understand," she said, leaning over to give Sadie as much a hug as the huge massage chairs would allow. "Whatever you decide, Sadie."

"I'll talk to Axel when we get back. Before the makeup session."

She'd likely cry it all off otherwise. Because she had a feeling this conversation wasn't going to go well.

Two hours later, her beach waves loose around her shoulders, Sadie texted Axel that she'd like to talk to him, that it was important. When she saw him, she'd speak the truth. No games. Just how she felt. She'd know in that moment. Right now, her mind was all over the place.

I'm actually at Daisy's house babysitting my nephew. Come over?

Be there in a few, she texted.

She sucked in a breath and headed up the path to the beautiful white farmhouse on the hill, where Axel had grown up a good portion of his childhood.

She walked up the porch steps, her heart suddenly beating so fast she wanted to just sit. But she knocked.

He came to the door, absolutely gorgeous, holding an adorable baby who couldn't be more than a few months old. He had big blue eyes—the Dawson eyes—and wispy brown curls and big cheeks. "This is Tony. Tony, meet the lovely Sadie Winston."

She managed a smile. "Hi, Tony. You sure are precious."

Another man, who looked a lot like Axel, came up behind him. "Hi, I'm this big lug's brother— Rex Dawson."

"Sadie Winston," she said, shaking his hand. "I'm sorry for barging in. I didn't realize Axel had company or that Daisy did." She shook her head, nothing coming out right. "We can talk later, Axel."

"No, now is fine," Rex said. "Trust me. I was just about to surprise Noah with my presence at the ranch—a rare occurrence. Back in thirty, Axel."

"Nice to meet you," Sadie said.

Rex smiled. "Likewise." He got in a buggy and drove off.

She and Axel made small talk for a minute or so about his brother, who was in town for only a few hours, and Tony and how the weather was terrific for a wedding.

"Speaking of," Sadie said, her heart now twisting.

The more she looked at Axel, particularly *this* Axel, with a baby in his arms, the more she knew she needed to let him go. Being a fake dad-to-be for Danny was fine for him, being a doting uncle was fine for him, but being a real dad wasn't. And Sadie needed a real husband, a real father for her son. She needed real love, big love.

She'd be her own date to the wedding.

"I think I should attend the wedding solo," she said. She stopped short of explanations since she knew none was necessary. He knew why.

"Oh," he said. "I feel bad about ruining the seating arrangements."

She glared at him. That was what he felt bad about?

Suddenly she realized how right her sister had been to tell Axel he was off the hook. That was how he looked at it, she realized. He just wanted to finish out the week because he cared about her and her family and at heart, he was a good guy.

Just not one in love with her.

She cleared her throat and ignored the stinging sensations in her eyes. "Evie has a blind date arranged for me—she's promoting one of Marshall's friends from the singles table to be my plus-one."

"Oh," he said again, staring at her. "So you have another date."

"Well, if I want. And to be honest, I don't want another date. You're a hard guy to top, Axel Dawson."

He stared at her, so many emotions in his eyes she couldn't read what he was thinking. "I'm sorry I can't be what you need," he said very solemnly. "I wish I could."

Dammit. "Oh, really?" she asked. "Because you do know it's up to *you*."

He rocked the baby in his arms. "It's not that simple."

"Then I guess this is goodbye," she said. "I have the wedding tonight and we're leaving after breakfast in the morning. I'll tell Danny you said bye and give him a hug for you."

He winced. "I'd like to do that myself. If that's all right."

"Fine. Because I know Danny would feel bad otherwise. We're leaving at eight sharp."

She looked at sweet Tony, then at the man holding him. And she turned and left before she completely fell apart.

Chapter Sixteen

Axel and Rex easily found 62 Bear Ridge Lane, which was right off Main Street, a three-family house with two balconies on the top stories. A woman in her early sixties was sitting on a chair on the porch, a small dog in her lap. She had a hard edge to her but was attractive with lots of wild auburn curly hair and dark brown eyes. She wore a lot of silver bracelets on both arms and a long sundress. The dog wore a hot-pink collar dotted with rhinestones.

"Cocker spaniel," Rex said to Axel. "Always loved the long, floppy ears."

Axel eyed his brother. "Should we ask if she knew Dad?"

"Excuse me, miss?" Rex called out from the walkway. The guy never waited. He just *did*—his MO. Not a bad trait, in Axel's opinion.

The woman peered at them. She didn't look particularly friendly.

"Did you know Bo Dawson?" Rex asked.

"Who's asking?" The woman grabbed a pair of glasses from the small round table beside her. She put them on, and her entire expression changed. "As I live and breathe. Honey Bear," she said to the little dog, hand to her chest, "do you know who these two men are? I do. Yes, I most certainly do. They've got to be Bo's kids."

"I'm Axel, and this is Rex."

She got up and put the dog down. Honey Bear came over to sniff their legs, then went up to the porch and curled up on a red floor pillow. "I heard all about you. The six of you. Five boys and a girl. Well, adults, of course. But Bo always referred to y'all as the kids."

"Your address was listed in a letter that my dad left me," Axel said. "Just a bunch of addresses, no notes about them. So we were wondering what your relationship was to Bo."

"Huh, interesting. Well, I'll tell you. I was his last girlfriend. My name is Nell. He dumped me out of nowhere, told me it was over, he was sorry but he was moving on, and I was devastated. I loved your dad something fierce. Next thing I know, I get a letter from him from beyond the grave—freaked me out. I knew he'd passed on and I couldn't imagine why I'd get a letter after. He asked the manager of the bar we used to go to to send it to me if anything ever happened to him."

Axel looked at Rex. His dad had been making amends all over town, it seemed.

"The letter was short and sweet. He said he'd been crazy in love with me but he was no good and didn't deserve me, that he'd wrecked everything meaningful in his life and he'd wanted us to part before that happened. He wrote that he knew he was dying and needed me to move on with a good man worthy of a woman like me. Do you believe that? Worthy of a woman like me. No one's ever said anything like that to me before." Tears came to her eyes. "I did eventually start dating again and about three months ago, I found my Mr. Right. We're going on a cruise next month."

"I'm sure Bo would be comforted to know that," Axel said.

"Your father was a lot to handle, but I would have cared for him till the end. If he'd let me. I feel so bad that he died alone, without a loving woman at his side. But I guess he had his kids there."

Rex nodded. "We were all there."

"Good," she said. "I loved him despite his flaws. I loved him as he was."

"I'm glad he had that in his thoughts," Rex said. "I'm sure it was comforting."

Honey Bear got up and started barking at two kids on bicycles.

"Oh, hush now," she told the dog. "I'd better get her inside. Day camp just let out."

Rex smiled at her. "Thanks for talking to us."

"Bye now," she said and scooped up Honey Bear.

Rex seemed mystified. "Wow."

Axel nodded. "What you said."

"He thought he was leaving her for her own good," his brother said as they headed up the sidewalk and turned the corner onto Main Street. Rex shook his head. "The notions we get in our head, right?"

Axel didn't respond to that.

Rex eyed him. "I think Dad's trying to tell you something, and just in time. There's a reason you finally opened his letter to you now."

That reason was Sadie.

He could feel something shift inside his chest, but he couldn't quite figure out what it meant.

"I've got to hit the road. I'll drop you off, then hit the airport. Kiss Tony, Chase and Annabel for me. I already miss my little niece and nephews."

"Will do," Axel said.

"Don't let her get away, Ax. Think long and hard but not too long. Things change fast. Trust me."

Sadie's beautiful face and Danny's adorable one floated into his mind, Zul the superhero lion in his hand, of course.

Again, there came that feeling, that movement in his chest, something happening. *Be the boss of yourself,* he heard the mountain man say, but suddenly, it meant something else. It meant not to let old wounds or bitterness or fear tell him what to do.

He needed to see Sadie. He needed to be with her and maybe he'd understand what the hell was happening inside him. Maybe it was all Nell had said. All the stories he'd heard from the people whose addresses had been on the list. Maybe it was Sadie and Danny themselves. Maybe it was everything.

He glanced at the clock on the dash of Rex's Jeep. It was 5:06 as his brother pulled up to Axel's cabin. The wedding had already started. In fact, Evie Winston and Marshall Ackerman were saying their vows right now.

Maybe that was a sign—that he should stay put at home with Dude.

Or maybe he had a wedding reception to crash.

Sadie had a waiter remove the place setting of her plus-one and scooted over a bit so that she'd have more elbow room. There. See, who said attending a wedding alone didn't have a silver lining? More space. At Sadie's table were her parents, her dad looking quite handsome in his suit, her grandparents, Aunt Tabby and Cowboy Joe, and Izzy. Danny and the other young kids were next door in the kid zone, where three ranch staffers were showing them a grand old time and getting paid time and a half. Izzy said she and Sadie would be each other's dates since that "handsome fiancé of yours obviously had a ranch emergency."

That was when Sadie sucked in a breath and told her great-grandmother, who at ninety-nine deserved not to be pandered to, the entire story. The truth.

Izzy's hazel eyes got misty. "You cared so much for my feelings that you and that tall drink of water pretended to be engaged all week? Why, that's the sweetest thing I ever heard."

A huge weight lifted off Sadie's chest. Izzy was the best. She hugged her great-grandmother, inhaling her trademark scent of roses. "I love you, Great-Gram."

"Love you, too, Sadie-girl," Izzy said.

A slow song started playing, "Fly Me to the Moon," one of Izzy's favorites, so Sadie asked her great-grandmother to dance. It involved pushing her in her wheelchair in little movements, but Izzy had a great time and sang along. Back at the table,

Sadie told her mom and grandmother that she'd come clean to Izzy, and they were glad to hear it.

One of Sadie's favorite songs started playing, a beautiful ballad. She sipped her wine and closed her eyes, wondering what Axel was doing right now. Playing fetch with Dude in the yard. Eating dinner alone. Out riding and not thinking about her at all.

"May I have this dance?"

Sadie gasped. Standing beside her was Axel in the flesh. Well, dressed, but very much there. He wore a gray suit and Stetson and was so gorgeous and sexy she couldn't speak for a second.

"You clean up well," was all she could manage to say.

"And you look absolutely beautiful," he said, taking in her beachy waves, which, of course, he'd seen earlier, and the mauvey-pink maid of honor dress that showed a bit more cleavage than Sadie was used to.

"Make a habit of crashing weddings, do you?" she asked, her heart hoping against hope that he was here because he couldn't live without her.

Maybe he was just passing by. *Yeah, Sadie—in a suit. In the lodge.*

He got down on one knee.

Sadie gasped again. She was aware of the table going silent.

Axel pulled out a black velvet box and opened

it, a stunning round diamond ring twinkling at her, baguettes on the side. "For real this time, Sadie. I love you and Danny with all my heart, and you'd make me very happy if you'll marry me."

Viv let out a small shriek. Vanessa grabbed her husband's arm. Izzy pressed her hand to her heart.

"Yes!" Sadie whispered, out of breath. "Yes, yes, yes." She flew into his arms, and he stood and lifted her, spinning her around and kissing her.

"Hey, what did I miss?" Evie asked, dancing over with her new husband.

"Oh, just this," Sadie said, holding out her hand.

Evie yelped and hugged her and then Axel. "I have the best evil ideas, don't I?" she whispered to Sadie.

Sadie laughed. "You certainly do."

Axel and Sadie danced every slow dance for the rest of the night, then hugged everyone goodbye and went to pick up Danny from the kid zone. The room had long turned into a *sleep* zone, and Axel carried a fast-asleep Danny out to his SUV. Turned out that Sadie and her little boy weren't leaving at eight sharp tomorrow morning, after all.

They were home.

Epilogue

Four months later...

Viv Winston gasped so loud in the doorway of the bathroom that her mother and sister came running, Izzy wheeling herself into the hallway to see what the fuss was.

Sadie, her sister, mother, aunt, grandmother and great-grandmother were over at Evie's house in Prairie City for their weekly Saturday lunch, where they gossiped and ate and laughed and had a grand old time for hours. Danny was there, too, in the play area Evie had long ago set up for visits from her favorite and only nephew.

Sadie and Evie burst into laughter as their mother, so emotional she couldn't speak, grabbed the two home pregnancy test sticks out of both her daughters' hands and held them up.

"I'm going to be a grandmother!" she screamed.

"I'm going to be a great-grandmother!" Vanessa screamed.

"I'm going to be a great-aunt!" Tabby shouted, clapping.

"I'm going to be a gray-gray-grandmother!" Izzy yelled, throwing her hands up in the air and waving them.

They all cracked up at that and Sadie and Evie left the bathroom, hugs and kisses and congratulations all around. They hadn't planned to be pregnant at the same time, but they'd talked about how great it would be if they were, and when Sadie had mentioned that she was late, Evie had said she was, too, and they'd run to the drugstore for matching tests.

Two plus signs.

"Should we have told our husbands before our relatives?" Sadie asked Evie.

"With this crew, are you kidding? You can't keep anything private. Hurry and tell Danny he's going to be a big brother before anyone beats you to it."

Sadie laughed. Viv was on the phone, making reservations at her favorite restaurant for that night—without even asking if anyone was free. Big news like this took precedence over plans anyone else had. And Vanessa was on the phone with her bridge and knitting clubs. Aunt Tabby was texting Cowboy Joe—their romance was still going strong, and Tabby had never seemed happier.

Izzy, meanwhile, called Sadie and Evie over. "Just to make double-decker definitely sure I heard right. You're *both* pregnant. Both."

Sadie chuckled. "Yes. Both. For real."

"I knew it would all work out, didn't I?" Izzy asked.

"You sure did," Sadie said.

After a big hug with Great-Gram and Evie and a wave to Viv and Vanessa, who were both still on the phone calling every person they knew, Sadie picked up Danny from his play area, Zul the superhero lion still his favorite toy. Just when Danny finally learned to say Axel, his hero had become his father and was now Daddy. Zul had stuck for the superhero lion, and Axel loved that.

"Guess what?" she told Danny as she put him in his car seat. "You're going to be a big brother. Mommy and Daddy are going to have a baby."

"Baby bwuther?" Danny asked.

"Or a baby sister."

"Or a baby Zul!" he said, bursting into laughter and flying Zul above his head.

Sadie laughed and backed out of the driveway.

You never knew. That was *her* motto these days. She couldn't wait to get home to the luxe log cabin on the edge of the Dawson Family Guest Ranch where she now lived with her sexy husband and Danny, *their* son. Axel had formally adopted him, the final court appearance just two days ago. And now he'd be a father again.

She couldn't wait to tell Axel the news. She had no doubt he'd be overjoyed. The wedding crasher who'd proposed to her at Evie's reception had become a true family man. The other day, Daisy had said that happiness radiated from him, and Sadie had teared up at that. It was absolutely true.

At their wedding two months ago, his brothers had been amazed at the changes in the former lone wolf. Sadie had finally met Zeke and Ford, more tall, muscular, dark-haired, blue-eyed Dawsons, and between her family and his, plus friends and coworkers, the wedding had been a big, happy affair. Sadie had worn the dress she'd fallen in love with in Your Special Day and her mother's wedding veil, which Evie had also worn for her wedding. For something borrowed, she'd worn Aunt Tabby's pearl earrings. For something blue, her grandmother's delicate sapphire necklace. Izzy had contributed the something old with her beautiful diamond bracelet, which her own mother had given her as a wedding present almost eighty years ago.

She pulled up to the cabin and took Danny out

of his car seat. "Want to tell Daddy the news about your baby brother or sister?"

"Yes!" he said.

Axel came out on the porch, smiling and waving. Danny, as always sprinted ahead, waving Zul the superhero lion.

"Big news!" Danny said.

"Oh yeah?" Axel asked, raising his eyebrow at Sadie.

"I big bruwtha!" Danny said.

Axel's eyes widened. He stared at Sadie, who nodded as tears filled her eyes.

He raced down the porch, his son in his arms, and wrapped his free one around her. "Our family is getting bigger?"

She nodded. "And a new little cousin on my side, too. Evie's also pregnant!"

"How'd I get so lucky?" he asked. "A great little boy and another child on the way."

"Zul sup hero," Danny said, flying him around. "Zul saves day!"

Axel hugged them both close. "Zul is the best. I owe him a lot."

"We have thirty minutes to ourselves before we're expected in town for dinner to celebrate," Sadie said.

"Just enough time to call Daisy and make her day. She'll text my brothers the news."

"I love our big combined family," she said. "And I love you."

He kissed her tenderly on the lips. "I love you, too. Both of you! All three of you," he added, touching a hand to Sadie's belly.

Then they headed inside, a forever family.

* * * * *

Don't miss Melissa Senate's next book,

The Cowboy's Comeback,

book two in the Montana Mavericks: What Happened to Beatrix? continuity.